In The Eye of the Storm is presented by Phoenix Daniels

✿ Created with Vellum

The work is dedicated to those that I have loved and lost.

Victoria grabbed her gym bag and keys and headed out the door. She looked over at Mrs. O'Malley's closed door and waited on the mean old lady to come out and frown at her. "Ha! Maybe Mr. O'Malley is in there putting it on her good," Victoria said as she laughed to herself.

Suddenly, Victoria realized that she had never actually seen Mr. O'Malley in the three years that she'd been living in the building. Maybe the mean old racist had him tied to the bed.

Victoria continued to laugh out loud as she made her way downstairs. Her unexpected phone call from Jack left her in a great mood. She'd tossed and turned all night. She couldn't stop thinking about him. He had made the entire night of the benefit magical. She had never experienced anything so hot and passionate. She was ecstatic that she didn't have to wait until Saturday to see him again, but she was more than a little nervous about this dinner party.

Victoria wondered why he wanted her to meet his mother so soon. She tried not to read too much into it and decided to just be happy to see him again. Since this is the age of the internet, she decided that she would Google him and see if anything came up. To her surprise, Jackson Storm, CEO of Storm Enterprises, was all over the internet.

There were hundreds of articles about the "gorgeous billionaire playboy" and even more photographs of him with different women on his arm.

Victoria couldn't help but feel like she was out of her league. She was hoping that he wasn't trying to add another notch to his bedpost, or worst, he was just trying to get the black experience.

There were so many racial stereotypes about black women being wild animals in bed and white men having a small penis. But what Victoria was gripping in the back of that limo certainly dispelled that stereotype. Victoria needed something to take her mind off Jack's impressive dick, so she decided on the Stairmaster.

She actually found herself skipping to her car. Yeah, that sexy ass man was doing wonders for her mood. When she made it to her car there was another rose and card under her windshield wiper. She grabbed the rose and the note.

It read: "I said mine!!!!!"

Victoria tossed them both to the ground, hopped in her car, and took off. She wondered if Dante seriously thought that they could just pick up where they left off. She wanted no part of that man. He was a prosecutor. They met in court and immediately started dating. He decided to switch sides since being a defense attorney was more profitable. He had become very successful.

They were together for four years, until she found out that he had been sleeping with his ex. The bastard was actually sleeping with her for six months before he proposed to Victoria. She was totally heartbroken, and his betrayal almost destroyed her. Now, she was totally and completely over him. Seeing him at the benefit sparked absolutely nothing, and she was grateful that she'd found out who he was before she married him. All Victoria wanted now was for Dante to stop leaving shit on her car and leave her the hell alone!

Victoria's thoughts switched back to Jack. She wondered what the mother of a "gorgeous billionaire playboy" was like. She was more than a little nervous, but all she could do was be herself and see how that worked out.

According to one of the articles online, Jack had two younger sisters. She wondered if they were going to be at the dinner party and how they would react to her. She was still obsessing about Jack when she pulled into the gym's parking lot. She found a spot and headed into the gym. A good workout was what she needed.

Minutes later, she was working up a sweat on the treadmill. She looked over at the damn near naked woman on the next treadmill. She had been turtle walking and talking on the phone for the last fifteen minutes. She clearly had no intention of getting winded. The lady had a face full of makeup and was wearing a liter of perfume.

"Well, we know why she's here," Victoria mumbled under her breath. Three hours later, Victoria stood in front of her closet trying to figure out what to wear. She decided on a green knee length halter dress. It showed the tiniest of cleavage and had a flirty flare at the bottom. It was sexy, but not too sexy. She didn't want Jack's mom and sisters to think she was a slut. She did, on the other hand, want Jack to like what he saw.

The dress was perfect for the look that she was going for. The car was going to be there to pick Victoria up in an hour, so she needed to step it up. She put her hair in rollers, wrapped a scarf around her head, and tucked it all under a shower cap. She jumped in the shower and the hot water instantly relaxed her. She showered quickly and hopped out. She dried herself and applied her favorite moisturizer. She dressed and applied some mascara and lip gloss. She never wore much makeup. She decided to wear her hair down. She tied a pretty pink and green scarf around the front and let the rest of her bouncy curls hang loosely. Now the shoes. Shoes were always the best part of any outfit. She chose a five-inch pink patent leather strappy sandal. They were gorgeous. Victoria could afford pretty, not Prada.

She wore the diamond studs that had been a gift from her mom for her thirtieth birthday. They were classy and beautiful. She misted herself with her favorite perfume, Rebel by Rihanna. She walked over to the floor-length mirror and checked herself out. She was pleased with her look, but still a little nervous. She had just decided to have a glass of wine to calm her nerves when the phone rang. She didn't recognize the number on the caller ID, but she answered anyway. "Hello?"

A male voice spoke: "Ms. Price, your car has arrived."

She thanked the driver and told him that she would be right down. She grabbed her keys and her purse and headed out the door, wishing for that glass of wine. This time, Mrs. O'Malley was front and center.

"Good evening, Mrs. O'Malley," Victoria said brightly.

The old lady looked her up and down. She muttered, "Um humph".

Then she slammed her door. Victoria vowed to never greet that cow again! Once outside, the driver was already holding the door open for Victoria. She took a deep breath and climbed inside. Sitting on the leather instantly took her back to the explosive orgasm that she'd had in that very seat, and she could feel her lady parts getting moist.

After fifteen minutes of driving, the limo stopped. Victoria looked out of the darkly tinted window and discovered that she was downtown. The door opened, and as the driver assisted her out of the limo, she realized that she was at Storm Enterprises. The driver led Victoria through the doors and into the massive lobby. "Right this way, Ms. Price."

Then he led her to a set of elevators. Victoria wondered if the dinner party would be held there. The driver ushered her into an elevator. He used a key card and pushed P. He stepped out of the elevator and said, "Enjoy your evening, Ms. Price."

Before the elevator door closed, she said, "Please call me Victoria or Vic." He nodded and the doors closed. When the elevator stopped and the doors opened, Victoria gasped at the vision before her. The sight of a breathtakingly handsome Jack standing in front of Chicago's beautiful skyline almost made Victoria stumble.

She slowly stepped from the elevator and into one of the most beautiful rooms that she'd ever seen. The room had all white furnishings with splashes of bright blues. The beautiful paintings were probably worth more than everything she owned. She peeled her eyes from the powerful sculptures and back to the beautiful man in front of her. He could easily grace the cover of GQ. His powerful gaze was almost intimidating. He was wearing an olive casual v-neck that revealed his impressive biceps and slacks that hung perfectly from his hips.

"Hi," barely escaped her lips.

The impression that Jack was making was breathtaking. He smiled and strolled over to Victoria. He wrapped his arms around her waist and pulled her into his body. He leaned in and kissed her softly on the lips and then he whispered in her ear.

"So beautiful." He pulled back, grabbed her hand, and led her to a bar that sat directly in front of the floor-to-ceiling window. "I thought you might like a drink before we head to my mom's." Even his voice did things to her body.

"I would love a glass of wine," she confessed with a smile, desperately needing something to take the edge off. Jack nodded with consent and walked behind the bar. He handed her a glass and grabbed a bottle of wine from the rack. He located a corkscrew, opened the bottle, and poured her a full glass. Jack chose a smaller glass, dropped in an ice cube, and poured an amber-colored liquid into his glass. He walked around the bar and sat next to Victoria. His scent overwhelmed her, making her weak in the knees. She silently thanked God that she was sitting.

"Victoria, you look beautiful," he said as he reached over and placed his hand over hers. "I know you're a little nervous about the dinner party, so I decided to get you liquored up first."

He signaled his humor with a wink.

"Good idea," Victoria replied with a giggle. "So, give me some intel. Tell me about your family."

Jack took a sip from his drink and gave Victoria the rundown on the Storm family. Victoria was surprised to learn that Jack didn't come from money. Well, not billions anyway. Both of his parents were attorneys who established their own very successful law firm. Jack's mother had retired from the firm, while his father pretended to retire but hadn't stopped sneaking into the office to check up on things.

She also learned that the oldest of Jack's little sisters, thirty-year-old Emily, followed in her parent's footsteps and was now running the firm. His twenty-eight-year-old baby sister, Amy, was an accountant and worked at Storm Enterprises. She was also gunning for the title of CFO.

Victoria was also surprised to hear that Jack built his business from the ground up. He had no desire to practice law. He wanted to build things. He'd bought his first property with money that he borrowed from a bank, not his parents. It was a three-unit apartment building with a storefront. The more Jack spoke, the more impressed Victoria became. "Your turn," he told her. "Tell me why the Sickle Cell Association is so important to you."

Victoria downed the last of her wine and placed her glass on the bar. She looked at Jack with sad eyes. "My niece, Delilah, has the disease. She's five years old and the most wonderful little girl in the world. She was diagnosed as a baby, and it broke my heart."

She explained that there was no cure for the painful debilitating disease. There are hardly any funds for research and treatment. Since children with Sickle Cell need very specific care, some aren't able to participate in the same activities as normal children. Victoria's dream was to raise enough money to build a summer camp equipped with a staff of doctors and nurses that were trained to care for children with the disease. "Delilah hasn't had a pain crisis yet. Most children have their first by four. My little angel is blessed."

"Yes, she is. She's blessed with a caring and beautiful aunt." Jack grabbed her hand and pulled her from her seat. He remained in his bar stool and positioned her between his legs. He hugged her tightly.

Victoria could feel his hard chest against her nipples. They instantly hardened. He loosened his grip and leaned in for a kiss. It started out soft and tender, but when his tongue touched hers, the kiss deepened. Her body was reacting, and she moaned into his mouth. His hands roamed her back and reached her backside. He pulled her closer, and his arousal was pressed into her stomach. Her panties were quickly getting wet.

Unexpectedly, Jack slowly eased Victoria back. He looked pained. "Victoria, if we don't stop now, we'll never make it to dinner," he said breathlessly.

He stood and adjusted his impressive package. Victoria stared desperately at the huge bulge in his pants, and her mouth watered. She looked up at him. He had a knowing smirk on his face. She laughed and turned to the window to admire his view. He stood behind her and wrapped his arms around her waist. Now his big dick was stabbing at her back. She chuckled and elbowed him lightly in his side. "Get away from me, you tease."

He laughed and pulled her towards the elevator. She followed while thinking how badly she needed a wet wipe. They made their way down the elevator and through the lobby to the waiting limo. They hopped in, and the driver closed the door. Victoria looked around the limo and then glanced over at Jack. He was wearing a sexy smirk, and her cheeks instantly heated. She knew that he was remembering their last time in the limo. He reached into his front pocket and pulled out her panties. Her eyes widened as he placed them to his nose. He put them back in his pocket and pulled Victoria to his lap. "You're so bad," she whispered into his ear.

"Baby, you have no idea." They laughed and teased each other during the entire ride. Thirty minutes later, they were heading uphill on a winding driveway.

Victoria slipped from Jack's lap and looked out the window. This was no house. It was a mansion! When the vehicle came to a stop, Victoria's nervousness returned. Jack gave her hand a reassuring squeeze, and they got out of the limo. They made their way up the walkway, and Jack rang the bell. They stood in the doorway, hand-in-hand. The door was opened by an older man in a uniform who, Victoria assumed, was the butler. She had never seen a butler outside of television shows. The man smiled brightly and shook Jack's hand. "Welcome home, Jackson." Then he gave Victoria a polite nod.

"It's good to see you, William," Jack responded with his own bright smile. William led them to what he called a parlor. Apparently, everyone else had already arrived and were enjoying a cocktail hour. Jackson and Victoria stepped into the beautifully decorated room. Victoria, still clinging to Jack's hand, looked around the elegant room at all of the smiling faces. A beautiful older woman looked towards the doorway and screamed, "Jackson!"

Everyone looked up at them, and all conversation immediately stopped. You could hear a mouse pissing on cotton in that room. Victoria looked around at all the shocked faces, and she was instantly mortified. The woman hurried over to Jack and Victoria. She reached up, grabbed Jack's face with both hands, and kissed his cheek. She looked over at Victoria and smiled, before bringing her in for a warm embrace. She whispered in Victoria's ear, "I'm sorry, dear. It's just... well... Jackson has never brought a woman home before." She released Victoria, looked up at Jack and then back to Victoria. "I'm Katherine, Jackson's mother. Welcome to my home."

Victoria exhaled, not realizing that she had been holding her breath. "Thank you, Katherine."

Jack cut in. "Mother, this is Victoria." "Well, aren't you lovely? Come with me so I can show you off." Then Katherine pulled Victoria from Jack's grasp. Katherine was still quite beautiful. She had salt-and-pepper hair that she wore short and spiky. She had the same ocean-blue eyes as Jack. She was wearing a striking cream pantsuit and had the nerve to be sporting a pair of beige, to die for, four-inch Christian Louboutin pumps.

"Everyone, this is Victoria, Jackson's girlfriend," Katherine happily announced. Victoria was a deer in the headlights. She looked back at Jack, and he had the nerve to wave goodbye. After what seemed like hundreds of introductions, a man that had to be Jack's father walked into the parlor. He stood as tall as Jackson. He had dark hair that was slightly gray on the sides. He made his way over to Victoria and Katherine. It was clear that Jack inherited his mother's eye color, because this man had emerald green eyes.

He approached and looked lovingly at Katherine. He gave her a tender kiss on her lips. Damn, he was fine! He reached for Victoria's hand, brought it to his lips, and spoke in a deep smooth voice. "And, who is this lovely young woman?"

"Darling, this is Jackson's girlfriend, Victoria," she answered breathlessly. It was clear that the man still swept her off her feet.

"Victoria, this flirt is Jackson's father, Joseph." Joseph smiled at Victoria. "Well, he certainly made a lovely choice."

"Yes, Father, I did, so stop kissing her," Jack said as he pulled Victoria to his side possessively. He reached out and shook his father's hand. Victoria was staring between the two men. The resemblance was uncanny. She forced herself to speak, "It's very nice to meet you, Joseph."

She looked over at Jackson and said, "You are the spitting image of your father, and you should thank him every day."

The group erupted in laughter. Jack's hold tightened on Victoria, and he was no longer laughing. His expression went cold, so Victoria followed his line of sight. It was her, "angry blonde."

Katherine turned to see what was affecting her son's mood and quickly turned back, rolling her eyes. "Angry blonde" hoisted her overexposed boobs up, plastered a fake smile on her silicone-filled lips, and approached the group. "Well, hello all," she said loudly.

Victoria was sure that she saw Jack's parents cringe. "Caroline," they responded in unison without looking at her.

"So, you've met Victoria," Caroline said in an even louder voice. Victoria realized that the bitch was trying to cause a scene.

Victoria noticed that the room had become quiet and the other dinner guests were staring. Caroline looked smugly at Victoria and announced loudly, "You do know that he paid a million dollars for her, don't you?"

Victoria gasped along with everyone else in the room. She was humiliated, and she wanted to run from the room. Actually, she wanted to beat the shit out of the stuck-up rich bitch, and then run from the room.

Jack looked as if he wanted to punch Caroline himself. Suddenly, a female voice from behind yelled out, "Well, it looks like she'll be getting about fifteen billion more out of the deal! Which is a hell of a lot more than the one night and lobster tail that you got!"

Victoria could actually hear laughter, and Caroline turned completely red when an older man, who Victoria assumed was her father, walked over and grabbed her by the arm. The man yanked her away. Victoria turned around to see the woman that defended her. She was walking in Victoria's direction. She was beautiful. She had long dark hair and piercing blue eyes. She was about five-nine with a gorgeous figure. She looked like a supermodel. She winked at Victoria and threw her arm over her shoulder. "Sorry, I'm late. Got caught up at the office." She directed her apology toward Joseph and Katherine. "Emily, it's Sunday," Katherine scolded. Victoria squeezed Emily's hand and said, "Thanks, Emily. I'm Victoria." "Yeah, I know. I heard Caroline from the front porch," Emily said laughing. She released Victoria and rushed Jack for a hug. She punched Jack on the arm and said, "I haven't seen this busy man in a month." He responded with, "Emily, no one works more than you." Emily actually managed to return the smile to Jack's face. William entered the room and announced dinner, so the crowd filed into the dining room. Victoria had never seen a dining room so opulent in someone's house. Gorgeous centerpieces filled with yellow and white lilies lined the extremely long dining room table. The seats were covered in luxurious white fabrics tied by bright yellow bows. Victoria was floored. She looked up at Jack, assuming that he was accustomed to such beauty. Surprisingly, he appeared to be just as impressed as Victoria. "Mom, this is beautiful." Victoria was now feeling a little less out of place. Jack led her to her seat and pulled out her chair. She sat and he took a seat next to her. Victoria leaned in and whispered to Jack. "Your mother is telling everyone that I'm your girlfriend." Jack smirked and whispered. "Good. It'll keep their gold-digging daughters away." They shared a private giggle, but Victoria shook her head. "I'm sorry, Mr. Storm, but that little girlfriend announcement just made you even more desirable." Jack looked briefly confused, but then confusion turned to mischief. He narrowed his eyes and asked, "So what you're saying is, all this time, all that I had to do to get women was get a girlfriend?" Victoria narrowed her eyes at him and punched his thigh under the table. They shared another laugh until their private moment was interrupted. "So, Jack, tell us how you come to purchase Victoria," asked a voice from across table. Jack and Victoria looked up to find a man smiling and staring directly at Victoria with what looked like desire. Jackson smiled at the man that she hadn't been introduced to. Something changed in Jack's demeanor. He became protective. He reached under the table, possessively placed his hand on Victoria's thigh, and put on his businessman's face.

Everyone at the table quietly awaited an answer, and Victoria couldn't wait to give them one. This was her chance to tell a bunch of rich folks about the Sickle Cell Association. She smiled brightly and explained the benefit and Jack's generous donation at the auction. She spoke passionately about the charity.

The dinner guests seemed genuinely interested and, by the end of the conversation, some even promised to write checks before the end of the evening. Jack leaned in and kissed Victoria on her forehead. Victoria noticed Joseph give Katherine a small nod. Katherine looked at Victoria with a smile filled with pride and approval.

Victoria began to feel as if she and Jack were being deceitful by allowing his parents to believe that they were in a committed relationship. She didn't much care what the other guests thought, but she didn't want to lead his family on. She became instantly uncomfortable and decided that she would ask Jack to come clean to his parents.

She quietly got through the rest of the dinner and, when it was over, the guests then returned to the parlor. Victoria stayed behind and walked over to the patio. She decided to step outside to get some air.

The Storm's patio was like being at the expensive luxury resorts that she'd seen on TV. It truly took her breath away.

"I have a million dollars," a voice said from behind.

Victoria turned to see the smiling man from dinner. He was an attractive man of about thirty-five. The man was impeccably dressed and stood at about six feet.

"Good for you." Victoria quickly responded and returned to the view. He moved beside her and said, "I'm Greg, Gregory Donovan."

"It's nice to meet you, Gregory Donovan."

Since he obviously wasn't going to allow her to enjoy her moment alone, she turned and walked towards the house. When she entered the patio doors she looked back and said, "Enjoy your million dollars."

She walked through the dining room and into the hall. Victoria said a silent prayer that she didn't get lost on her way to the parlor.

"Wait!" Gregory was calling her from behind, but she kept walking. "I didn't mean to offend you," she heard him say. He sped up his pace and caught up to her just as she entered the parlor. He continued with, "I figured since you're just Jack's charity, you wouldn't mind hanging out with me."

Victoria's steps haltered and again all eyes were on her. Caroline smiled victoriously. Victoria looked at Jack. His expression was murderous. Katherine and Emily looked sympathetically at her. Wondering if she was really Jack's charity, she stumbled backwards with embarrassment.

Victoria decided that she didn't belong there. She just didn't fit. She turned and hurried for the front door. She heard Katherine call her name. Then she heard what sounded like glass breaking. But she didn't look back. In fact, she started running. She ran from the front door and headed down the winding driveway.

After fifteen minutes of walking, Victoria had to remove her shoes.

The driveway had to be about three miles long. Every time she saw headlights she hid behind a tree.

Victoria didn't want to be found. Jack had called her repeatedly, but she'd just hit the ignore button. She wasn't mad at him. She just didn't want to talk. She didn't share his lifestyle. Maybe he did just want to get his money's worth for his donation.

She dialed Deon's number and prayed for an answer. When she heard his voice, she thanked God. She sat on a rock outside of the Storm's property, hidden from passing vehicles. Thirty-five minutes later, she was sitting in Deon's car avoiding all conversation. She didn't want to talk. Deon gratefully didn't push.

IN THE EYE OF THE STORM

PHOENIX DANIELS

CHAPTER 1
KATHERINE

Katherine ran down the hall, strangely eager to be on time for her least favorite class.

Once she arrived at the classroom, she slowed her labored breaths, opened the door, and entered her ethics class.

Ethics should have been a given, not a course.

The course study was tedious, commonsensical, and a waste of a good hour. Her second year of law school was proving to be the longest year of her life, and she had a handful of more classes that she'd deemed unnecessary.

She entered the room; thankful her professor wasn't there. After hurrying to her seat, she pushed her long, dark hair out of her face and fished a pen and a notebook out of her backpack.

"You made it," came from Laverne, her friend since high school. Hers and Laverne's parents were longtime friends. They'd grown up in the same affluent neighborhood and attended the same private school. Both families were core members of Chicago's wealthy and elite.

"I know. Professor Campbell kept me in her office forever. She's not pleased that I haven't sought out an internship with Harvey and Payne."

Laverne leaned forward and rested her chin in her hand. "Why haven't you? With your grades and your family's connections, you can get an internship anywhere."

Katherine shrugged. Larry Crane's family of bankers basically ran the law firm of Harvey and Payne. His dad was good friends with the managing and senior partners. It was bad enough that her parents had practically promised her to Larry. The last thing she needed was to be working at a law firm where his family had so much influence.

"Are you going to Nate's party tonight?" Laverne asked, thankfully changing the subject.

"Can't. It's my parents' anniversary. They're having a cocktail party, and I've been told my presence is mandatory."

"Ugh, bummer."

Laverne was right. It was a bummer.

Katherine hated her parents' social gatherings. Their events promised a night of pretending to listen to boring stories told by shallow, pretentious people. The company her parents kept was telling.

While she loved her parents, they were out of touch. They lived in a wealthy bubble of excess with no care or concern for the outside world. She was grateful for the life of privilege they'd given her, but she was determined to form her own path in life. She wanted to help people, which was why she decided to place her focus on civil rights and constitutional law.

Damn!

The sound of her stomach growling pushed all thoughts of her parents out of her head.

Katherine covered her stomach with her hand and looked around to see if anyone had heard. Judging by Laverne's smirk, she had.

"Damn, Kate," she said with a giggle. "Didn't you have breakfast?"

Katherine shook her head. "Didn't have time. I was running late, but I'm gonna grab something from the vending machine."

Laverne made a face and Katherine understood why. The vending machine was stacked with stale chips and fossilized candy bars, and she wasn't looking forward to either, but she clearly needed to put something in her stomach.

"Good morning, ladies and gentlemen. Let's get started."

Katherine looked up to find Professor Grant standing in front of the classroom.

She scoffed and opened her textbook. Since the good professor had been hitting on her since the day they met, she found it ironic he was teaching ethics.

JOSEPH

Joseph walked through the sea of students. His destination was trademark law. Less than two hours ago, he was working on the assembly line at Ford Motor Company. Unlike a lot of the students at the University of Chicago, he needed to work. He also needed to sleep, but slumber would have to come later. He had responsibilities. Even though he wasn't an only child, he had his mom to take care of.

His twin brother, Jonathan, studied business at Harvard University and was just as passionate as Joseph about making sure their mother wanted for nothing. As a single parent, she struggled to make sure the two of them had everything they needed to succeed in life.

Their mother, Emily, taught history at an elementary school, and having an educator as a mom left no room for shenanigans. Education was no joke in their house, and furthering their education was *not an option* in Emily's eyes.

"You will get that piece of paper," she would often say.

So, Joseph and Jonathan had no choice but to take their studies seriously. And since Jonathan had opted to go to school in Massachusetts, Joseph felt he needed to stay close to home. Someone needed to stay with their mom. Besides, as far as law schools went, the

University of Chicago ranked in the top ten. Studying there was not only convenient but advantageous.

"Hey, Joe," Cynthia purred as he passed her.

"Hi," Joseph responded dryly. Not many people called him Joe.

He wasn't trying to be rude, and it wasn't that he was altogether uninterested. Cynthia was a pretty blonde with big tits who was highly coveted by the guys at school, but he didn't have time for highly coveted, big titty blondes. He needed to finish school and pay off the loans his mom had taken out for him and his brother's education.

Cynthia turned and caught his arm. "Are you going to Nate's party tonight?" she asked.

"Maybe. If I get my homework done, I might."

She smiled and pushed her breasts against his arm. "You're always so serious, Joe. Live a little."

Joseph smiled, pulled his arm from her grasp, and continued down the hall. "I'll try," he said over his shoulder.

Because of his schedule, he didn't have many friends. Nate was one of very few, and he'd promised to show up to Nate's birthday party. He considered himself a man of his word, so he intended to make an appearance.

"Shit!"

Joseph attempted to ignore the dark-haired woman banging on the vending machine, but her beauty wouldn't allow him to move on. The debutante, Katherine Chase, was nothing short of breathtaking. Still, he would never approach her. She was a legacy and, in his mind, a spoiled trust fund baby. Katherine was smart, but she didn't really have to be. No matter how good or bad she did in school, she would be fine. She was a Chase. Surely, there was no hustle, no struggle inside her. But hustle or not, Katherine was exquisite with her beautiful blue eyes and a body ripe for sin.

Joseph grabbed the vending machine and shook it until her candy bar fell to the bottom. Katherine looked up at him with a wide-eyed, hypnotizing gaze.

"Thanks," she said, batting long, dark lashes at him.

He pulled the candy bar from the bottom of the machine and frowned. "You shouldn't be eating this shit."

Katherine sighed. "I missed breakfast."

Joseph moved closer. She was *beautiful.* He wanted to cup her face in his hands and press his lips to hers. Unfortunately, those actions could get him kicked out of school.

Instead, he handed her the candy and continued down the hall.

"Thanks again," she said at his back.

"You're welcome," he told her without turning around.

Katherine had the face of an angel with the most beautiful blue eyes and plump, kissable lips. On more than one occasion, he'd found himself visualizing her full lips wrapped around his cock. Yet, no matter how smart and beautiful she was, he couldn't get distracted by the spoiled rich girls at his school.

As far as riches went, Katherine's family had an abundance of wealth. Her dad, Robert Chase, was a descendant of the super-wealthy Durst family, and his wife's family made millions in media. According to Forbes Magazine, the Chases were worth hundreds of millions of dollars, and if Joseph wanted to make even a fraction of that, he needed to stay focused.

CHAPTER 2
KATHERINE

Katherine entered the parlor and frowned at the lot of folks she didn't want to be spending her Friday night with.

"You look beautiful, Pumpkin."

She cringed at the sound of her dad's voice.

As her parents approached, her mother narrowed her eyes and handed her a glass of champagne. "It wouldn't hurt you to smile," she commented.

Katherine graced her mother with the fakest sugary smile. "There, you happy?"

"Hardly ever," her mother muttered before walking away.

"Be nice. Go mingle," her dad instructed.

Katherine downed the contents of her glass and then handed it to her dad. Sighing, she took off to mingle. Being social was basically her job. Her parents supported her financially, and she helped maintain their image of the perfect American family. It was a sort of partnership.

She scanned the room for someone she disliked the least. Unfortunately, her eyes landed on Larry, and he was headed her way.

"What's up, Kate?"

"Larry," she greeted dryly.

Because of his wealthy family, her parents thought of Larry as a great catch. They had no idea what a slimeball he actually was. Sure, he was tall and somewhat good-looking, but he was also a bully and a raging alcoholic.

"Fancy meeting you here."

Katherine ignored the corny line and walked over to the bar where Gabby, their housekeeper, was tending.

"Hey, Katie. Pinot?" Gabby asked.

"Yes, thank you."

Gabby poured a glass of pinot noir and handed it to Katherine. "How are you holding up? I know you hate these things."

Katherine rolled her eyes "I just gotta smile at people for an hour. That's how long it'll take for our esteemed hosts to get drunk enough not to notice that I've left."

Gabby laughed and held the bottle over Katherine's glass. "Let me top you off."

Katherine flinched at the feel of a hand on the small of her back. She turned and came face to face with her father. She reached back and slapped his hand away. Katherine could tell that he was feeling no pain. That was usually when things went bad.

"How are you drunk already?"

He looked from her to Gabby, and his fear of causing a scene made him throw his hands up in surrender. "Okay, Katie. I'll just go find your mother."

"Yeah, you do that," Katherine grumbled.

She rolled her eyes and turned her back to him. For now, she had no means of supporting herself or paying for school. However, as soon as she was able, she planned to run as far as she could without looking back. In her mind, she'd earned every penny her parents had spent on her.

"Katie, can you grab me a couple of bottles of merlot from the cellar?"

"Sure," Katherine agreed with a smile. She was grateful for any task that got her out of mingling with a bunch of people she had nothing in common with other than wealth.

Katherine weaved her way through the crowd, greeting folks as she left the parlor. After a long hallway, she took the stairs down to the cellar. Her father's wine cellar was his pride and joy, but it was her salvation. If she wasn't hiding from her folks, she was pilfering very old and very expensive wine.

After grabbing a basket from the island and hooking it on her arm, she walked over to the reds and collected four bottles of Tuscan merlot.

"Fancy."

Katherine turned toward the familiar voice and frowned when her eyes landed on Larry. "I'm sure you have a similar situation over at Casa de Crane."

"Something like this, but not as well-stocked," Larry admitted with a smirk.

"I'm sure you have a lot to do with that," Katherine quipped.

She moved to walk past him, but he grabbed her arm. He tried to lead her to a corner, but she resisted.

She didn't like being handled.

"Get your hand off me!" she demanded.

"Come on, Kate. Why are you always so combative?"

Katherine narrowed her eyes and used her free hand to push him away. "I don't like you, Larry."

Larry placed his face uncomfortably close to hers. "Well, you better start liking me because I'm your future."

She caught a whiff of the alcohol on his breath and moved toward the stairs. Larry could be a monster when he was drunk.

Before she reached the first step, he grabbed her by the elbow.

"Come here. Pay me some attention."

"Fuck you, Larry!" Katherine spat. "Don't touch me! You're not my goddamned future!"

He wrapped his fingers around her arm and pulled her against him. "Watch how you speak to me, Katie!"

"Go to hell, Larry!"

She snatched away from him and stomped up the stairs.

To hell with her parents' party. Larry's presence was all she needed to get the hell out of there. She was completely grossed out enough to make her escape.

CHAPTER 3
KATHERINE

Katherine turned the knob and entered the Gold Coast mansion. She walked through the foyer, greeting the few people she recognized. The crowd thickened when she entered the living room.

"You made it!" Laverne squealed, moving toward her with open arms, grinning from ear to ear, happy to see her. And very drunk. "What about your parents' party?"

"I ditched it."

Laverne laughed unusually loud and threw a heavy arm around Katherine's shoulder. "Atta girl!" she slurred. "Come on. Let's get you a drink."

Laverne pulled her toward the kitchen where they found a table holding a keg of beer and several bottles of wine. Since she was in a beer kind of mood, Katherine filled a disposable cup, took a sip, and trained her ear on the soft jazz floating in the air. She sang along with the lyrics of one of her favorite songs.

"Every child belongs to mankind's family

Children are the fruit of all humanity
Let them feel the love of all the human race
Touch them with the warmth, the strength of that embrace."

"CHILDREN OF SANCHEZ," CAME FROM BEHIND HER.

The familiarity of the deep, masculine baritone made her skin warm.

Katherine turned around and looked into a beautiful set of flawless emeralds. Joseph Storm was the kind of man that could stop a girl's breath—tall, muscular, and ridiculously handsome. And, on top of everything else, he smelled delicious.

"Hi, Joseph," she greeted shyly. "You know Chuck Mangione?"

Joseph nodded with a slight grin. "Yes, ma'am. I am a fan."

Katherine smiled. "Me too."

She gestured toward the table. "Drink?"

Joseph raised his cup to show her he already had a drink.

"Oh." Katherine lifted her cup to her lips.

Laverne leaned on her shoulder. "I'm gonna go umm... somewhere else," she whispered loudly before stumbling away.

"Are you friends with Nate or are you a party crasher?" Joseph asked.

"Been friends since the 5th grade. How about you?"

"We met when we were 17."

Katherine frowned. "High school?"

She didn't remember him from their school. Joseph had a face you didn't forget. There was no way he'd walked through the halls of Lake Forest Academy without her noticing him.

Joseph chuckled. "No. We didn't go to high school together. We met when he stole my girlfriend."

Unfortunately, she'd been mid-sip when he revealed how he and

Nate met because she found herself spitting beer. She quickly covered her mouth and grabbed a napkin from the table.

"You okay?" Joseph asked.

Katherine nodded frantically and wiped her mouth, completely embarrassed. "Sorry," she whispered, wiping beer from his shirt.

Joseph caught her hand and smiled. "It's okay."

The feel of his hand on hers gave her goosebumps.

Katherine looked up at him through narrowed eyes. "How could Nate steal a girl from you?" she asked suspiciously.

Nate wasn't a bad looking guy, but Joseph was a god. He couldn't have looked that much different in high school.

Joseph shrugged. "He's rich, and I'm not."

She chuckled. "Well, there you have it," she joked, but she couldn't begin to understand a girl that would dump a guy as gorgeous as Joseph because he wasn't wealthy. He was in law school, at the top of his class, and had a bright future in front of him.

❧

Fifteen minutes and two beers later, Katherine was still in the kitchen talking to Joseph Storm. Maybe it was the beer, but she found him very easy to talk to. She learned that he had a twin brother at Harvard Business School, and she admired the way he smiled when he spoke of his mother.

"Why law school?" he asked.

Katherine sighed. "To be honest, it started as a rebellion against my parents."

Joseph squinted as if he didn't understand. "*Law school* was your rebellion? What kind of rebellion is law school?"

She laughed uncomfortably. "My parents would much rather have me uneducated and married to a rich asshole." After a shrug, she added, "Like my mom."

Joseph opened his mouth to say something but changed his mind and pressed his lips together in a frown.

Katherine was starting to feel like she'd said too much. She was talking about rich people's problems to a man who had to work a full-time job while going to law school. He must've thought she was an overprivileged brat, and maybe she was.

She cleared her throat and placed her cup on the table. "I need to find the ladies' room. Excuse me."

She hurried out of the kitchen and turned down a hall, remembering that the bathroom was on the right. Luckily, someone came out as soon as she walked up. She slipped inside and turned to close the door, but she was met with resistance. On the other side of the door was Larry, wearing an angry scowl. He pushed her back and slammed the door closed before she could exit.

"Larry, what the hell are you doing?"

He moved close enough for her to smell the alcohol on his breath. "So, you're slutting around with the help."

Katherine rolled her eyes. "What do you mean, 'the help'? Joseph goes to the same law school that we go to."

"No doubt, on a scholarship. Surely, he can't afford the tuition," Larry said with a snide smirk.

Katherine matched his smirk. "More proof that he's a hell of a lot smarter than you. Without your daddy's money, you wouldn't have even been accepted into the University of Chicago."

Larry's bloodshot eyes went dark.

Her instincts warned her to get out of the bathroom.

Katherine shoved his chest, but he didn't move. Instead, he grabbed her by the throat and pushed her against the wall. Panic rushed over her as his fingers pressed her flesh. She struggled to breathe, but not because he was choking her. She was having a panic attack. Larry's touch was taking her to a dark place.

"Please," Katherine gasped, clutching his fingers. "Please, don't touch me."

She wanted to fight, but she was frozen in place. Her brain couldn't force her body to act, and she could feel herself getting lightheaded. Her vision blurred, and she was beginning to see red spots. Her body went limp, and the only thing keeping her on her feet was Larry's hand around her neck. Suddenly, she no longer had even that.

Katherine fell limp to the floor and did her best to rise onto all fours. She inhaled a deep breath and blinked until she could focus. She pushed her hair out of her face just in time to see Joseph Storm slamming Larry's face into the bathroom sink.

Larry let out a loud yelp and fell to the floor in a puddle.

With no more thought to Larry, Joseph turned around and lowered to his knee. When he reached out to touch her shoulder, Katherine jumped and slapped his hand away.

Joseph retracted his hand and held both hands up in surrender. "Are you okay?" he asked.

Katherine nodded. "Sorry."

She swiped a tear from her face and used the edge of the wall to help her stand.

"I'm fine," she said through a shaky breath.

With a worry in his eyes, Joseph reached out slowly to help.

"Don't," Katherine warned, raising her hand. She willed herself to her feet. Once she had secure footing, she pushed off the wall and scurried out of the bathroom.

CHAPTER 4
JOSEPH

After countless winding roads, Joseph pulled into the driveway of the Chase family's Bolling Brook mansion and stopped at the intercom. Since it was after midnight, he was hesitant to push the call button.

Katherine had run out of Nate's house in a hurry, leaving her purse behind. He could easily have given her purse to her friend, Laverne, but he didn't. Instead, he talked Laverne into giving him Katherine's address.

He wanted to lay eyes on her. The terror in her beautiful eyes when he'd tried to touch her had left him more than concerned. Understandably, Larry's behavior was deplorable. But after seeing Katherine cowering on the floor like a child, he believed there was so much more going on. There was definitely something bubbling beneath the surface.

Joseph wasn't going to lay eyes on her by staking out her driveway, so he pushed the button. After about a minute, a woman answered in a groggy voice. "Can I help you?"

He cleared his throat. "Joseph Storm to see Katherine."

"Joseph Storm?" The woman repeated his name like she thought he was lying.

"Yes, Joseph Storm."

"Joseph Storm, it's 12:17 PM."

Joseph looked down at his watch. "I'm aware of that, ma'am. I'm returning something that belongs to Miss Chase. If she's not available, I can try again at another time."

After a brief pause, the woman on the other end instructed him to stand by.

He waited patiently for four minutes. After that, as he contemplated leaving and reached up to put his 75 Ford Maverick in reverse, the gate opened.

Joseph drove through the gate and rounded the circular driveway until he was pulling up to the front door. Before he could get out of his car, the door opened. Light from the inside the house illuminated the walkway, revealing a female silhouette.

He climbed out of his car and made his way to the front door, and it was then that he noticed it was Katherine in the doorway. She was no longer wearing the same clothing she had on at the party. She was in sweats and a t-shirt, and her face had been washed clean of all makeup. He'd thought it was impossible, but she was even more beautiful. Her fresh face made her look more angelic than before.

"Joseph?"

Joseph took a few steps to meet her at the door.

"Hey. What are you doing here?"

He noticed she was trying to avoid eye contact as if she was embarrassed.

He moved closer and held out her handbag. "You forgot your purse."

Still with no eye contact, Katherine grabbed her purse. "Thank you," she said softly.

Joseph didn't at all like her behavior. He didn't know Katherine very well, but every time he was in her presence, she seemed strong and powerfully intelligent. Not at all like this timid woman scared to look him in the eye.

"Do you want to come in?" she asked, stepping to the side.

Joseph nodded. "I do."

He crossed the threshold and looked up at the tall ceiling and giant crystal chandelier as he waited for her to close the door.

"Follow me," she instructed, leading him across the foyer.

They took a hall and walked through an archway that led to a large room with plush leather furniture, a big wooden bar, and large leather chairs that could've been found in an ultra-exclusive gentlemen's club.

"Would you like a drink?"

Joseph followed her to the bar and took a seat on one of the fancy stools while Katherine walked behind the bar to fix drinks.

"What's your poison?" she asked.

"Any bourbon will do," he responded, realizing she probably had the best.

She pulled a tumbler from an overhead rack and placed it in front of her. "Ice?"

"No, ma'am."

After a two-finger pour, Katherine slid the glass over. She poured herself a glass of red wine, the whole time still not looking him in the eye.

"Katherine, I insisted on bringing your purse because I was worried. Are you okay?"

She sighed and practically inhaled the entire contents of the glass. When she finished her wine, she placed the glass on the bar and looked him in the eye for the first time that night. When she opened her mouth to speak, her focus shifted to something over his shoulder and her entire expression changed. All of a sudden, she was the same scared girl on Nate's bathroom floor.

Joseph turned and looked over his shoulder just as a pudgy, older man in a tacky satin robe entered the room. His thinning hair was a mixture of black and gray. Joseph placed his glass on the bar and stood to greet the man he assumed was Katherine's father.

"What's this?" the man asked.

"Dad, this is Joseph Storm. He goes to my school," Katherine introduced.

Her shaky tone prompted Joseph to turn and look at her. She appeared unstable, almost to the point where Joseph wanted to pull her into the protectiveness of his arms. Reluctantly, he tore his eyes away from her and walked over to her dad with an extended hand.

"Joseph Storm," he repeated.

Katherine's dad looked him up and down and stared at his hand a few seconds before accepting. "Robert Chase," he returned.

"It's nice to meet you, Mr. Chase."

Katherine's dad had a firm handshake, but it felt forced—like the insecurity of the smaller man.

"It's late, Joseph Storm," he pointed out with a frown.

"I realize that, sir. I came to return Katherine's lost purse."

Her dad's brow knitted, and he looked to Katherine. "Lost where?"

Joseph turned to Katherine, curious as to how she would answer, but the look in her eyes gave him pause. She seemed completely repulsed by her father's presence. Joseph couldn't help but wonder if she was still affected by what had occurred at Nate's, or if she was really repulsed by her own father. He didn't have a father, but when he had, his father had never looked at him like that.

Well, he had.

Once.

KATHERINE

As if her dad's presence wasn't bad enough, the pretentious way he was eyeing Joseph was utterly disgusting. Joseph had risen to greet him with a handshake. He was very polite. Yet, her dad looked at him like he was trash. Katherine had had enough.

"I lost it at school. Your presence is not necessary. You can go back to bed," she told him. She stepped out from behind the bar and grabbed Joseph's hand. "Come with me."

She practically dragged him out of the parlor and down the hall. They went through the kitchen, out a set of patio doors, and she led him to a furniture set that was well-lit by the lights in the swimming pool.

Katherine took a seat on the patio chair and welcomed Joseph to the chair next to her. He sat and crossed one long leg over the other. Now that she had him away from her father, she didn't quite know what to do or say next.

"It seems you don't like your father very much." His bold words killed the awkward silence.

Katherine chuckled and shook her head. "No, I don't like my father very much." She forced a smile and shifted uncomfortably in her seat.

"What about you? Do you like your dad?" she asked before he could ask her why she didn't like her father.

Sadness flashed in his eyes so fast that had she not been staring into his beautiful eyes, she would have missed it.

"My father is dead."

"I'm sorry, Joseph."

"It's fine," he responded with a wave. "It was a long time ago."

"Well, your mom sounds like a great person."

Joseph smiled. Joseph hardly ever smiled. The sight of his plump, sexy lips, framing brilliant white teeth nearly caused her to swoon.

"She is," he responded euphorically. "My mom is great."

Katherine felt an instant pang of envy. The feeling he seemed to get when thinking of his mother was foreign to her. Nothing about Elizabeth Chase elicited the warm and fuzzies. To say their relationship was strained would be an understatement. Her mother was shallow, superficial, and oftentimes, very cold.

Joseph's smile faded, and he frowned as if reading her thoughts. "You don't like your mom, either?"

"I could say I did, but it would be a lie," Katherine responded honestly.

Joseph parted his lips. She knew he was about to inquire about her relationship with her parents, so she cut him off with, "But, a twin, huh?" The thought of two tall, dark, and handsome specimens of perfection was exciting. "That must've been interesting growing up."

"Not as much as you'd think." Joseph chuckled. "He got me in trouble a lot."

Katherine smiled. It must've been nice to have a sibling. Growing up, she often wished she had a big brother to protect her from the monster under the bed.

Joseph looked down at his watch. When his eyes returned to her, a feeling of sadness washed over her because she knew he was preparing to leave.

"It's late. I should go."

Katherine stood, quickly and uncoordinated. "Oh?"

Joseph stood, considerably more gracefully. "I just wanted to bring you your purse." He turned toward the patio door and took one step before turning back. "That's not exactly true," he admitted. "You seemed distraught at Nate's. I really wanted to see if you were okay."

Katherine chuckled nervously. "I-I'm fine. I just... well... Larry... he's repulsive."

Joseph's brows wrinkled. "I thought you guys were friends. Honestly, the way he describes your relationship, one would assume you were more than friends."

"Larry Crane is a lying dirtbag!" Katherine spat, unable to hide her disgust at the thought of any kind of relationship with Larry.

Joseph laughed and threw his hands up in submission. "I stand corrected."

He turned and moved toward the patio, but Katherine grabbed his hand. His warm skin sent a jolt of fire through her veins. Joseph froze in his tracks and glared down at her hand before looking her in the eye. The emotion swimming in his vivid green gaze was an affirmation that he felt it too.

"Thank you," she whispered once she found her voice.

Joseph moved closer and caressed her elbow. "You're welcome."

His deep, sincere baritone was a hum to her core. Katherine had to force herself from pushing her body against his muscular frame. She wanted to slip her arms around his neck and force him into a passionate kiss that would convince him to take her right there on the patio. Instead, she released his hand and pointed to a pathway at the side of her house.

"You can go out this way," she told him, hearing the regret in her voice.

Joseph nodded and walked toward the path.

Katherine watched his back until he disappeared around the house. Then she stood, wishing she'd stopped him. But what would she have said if she had? After about a minute, she forced her feet to move. She turned toward the house and froze when she discovered her father watching her from a window in the kitchen. A shiver ran down her spine at the thought of him spying on her. Katherine frowned, rolled her eyes, and stormed into the house, wishing she had different parentage.

CHAPTER 5
JOSEPH

Joseph groaned and rolled over, trying to avoid the sun beaming through the window of his childhood bedroom. He suddenly remembered where he was when his body jerked from nearly falling off the tiny twin bed. After flipping the linen off, he sat up and glared at the window, recalling that he'd closed the shades before going to bed. His mom must have raised them. When they were younger, it was her way of waking him and his brother in the morning.

Joseph smiled. Some things never changed.

He grabbed his t-shirt from the floor and pulled it over his head. In a t-shirt and boxers—his normal breakfast attire—he left the bedroom and followed the smell of bacon.

"Good morning, sweetie," his mother greeted when he entered the kitchen.

She was at the stove, stirring something in a pot. Her long dark hair was pulled into a ponytail. She smiled at him with a sparkle in her bright blue eyes. For a woman with two grown sons, she was still so beautiful.

Joseph walked over and kissed the top of her head. "Good morning, Mom. Whatcha cooking?"

"Well, I have some oatmeal here," she said, waving toward the pot. "I scrambled a few eggs, fried some bacon, and I have biscuits in the oven."

Joseph inhaled the delicious aroma and moaned. "You're the best mom in the world."

"So, I've heard," she teased with a chuckle. "What are you doing here?"

He had his own apartment, but he sometimes slept over his mother's on Saturday nights so he could wake up and have breakfast with her on Sunday mornings.

Joseph raised a brow. "Can't I come see my favorite girl?"

"Anytime you want, sweetheart," she said with a smile. "Go and wake your brother. He's in his room."

Joseph squinted at his mom. "Jon is here?"

"He drove in this morning. Got in around four."

Joseph gave her another kiss before leaving the kitchen. He took the hall to his brother's room, opened the door, and found Jonathan buried under the covers.

Joseph walked over and yanked the blanket off his twin's head. "Get up!" he shouted, absent of all delicacy.

Jonathan rolled over, burying his head under his arms. "Fuck off," his brother grumbled.

Joseph laughed and pulled Jonathan's arm from his face. "What are you doing here? Don't you have finals?"

Jonathan had final exams all week.

"We completed our finals Friday. Can't a man visit his family?"

Joseph chuckled and plopped down on the bed, next to his brother. "How'd you do?"

Jonathan rolled over and looked at him with wrinkled brows. "You know how I did," he said, as if his success should have been obvious.

It was. Jonathan was the ultimate overachiever. Like Joseph, when it came to their education, he did everything exceptionally well.

"Mom made breakfast. She told me to wake you up."

Jonathan forced himself to sit up. "Gimme a minute. Let me brush my teeth." He frowned at Joseph. "May I suggest you do the same?"

Joseph blew hot breath into his hand and groaned. His brother had a point. So, he got up and made his way to the bathroom in his bedroom. He needed to get his toothbrush and wash the previous night from his mouth.

On his way to his bedroom, Joseph stopped in the kitchen and peeked in on his mom. She was still in front of the stove, but she was staring into space with a dolefulness he'd seen many times since his father's death. Guilt and shame warmed his face because he knew he was the cause of her sadness.

"Hey, Mom?"

His mother snapped out of her daze and turned to him with a rehearsed smile. "Yeah, sweetheart?"

"How would you like to go to Cape Cod for dinner tonight?"

Her eyes widened with excitement, but instead saying yes, she said, "You can't afford that."

Joseph smiled and walked over to his mom. He wrapped his arms around her and kissed the side of her face. "Why don't you let me worry about that, young lady?"

"Okay," she agreed with a giggle.

The Cape Cod inside the Historic Drake Hotel was her favorite restaurant, but his mother was right. Normally, he couldn't afford the upscale restaurant; they'd only gone for very special occasions. But he desperately needed to see a smile on her face. Tonight, he'd simply have to make a few sacrifices. Hopefully, his brother was willing to pitch in.

KATHERINE

"Good morning, Miss Chase," their daytime housekeeper greeted.

"Good morning, Diana," Katherine returned. She took a seat at the table, to the left of her mother. In their house, breakfast at the table was an unfortunate requirement. Thankfully, the food was always delicious. Garland, the chef, was beyond exceptional.

Knowing that she was preparing to speak, Katherine rolled her eyes at the sound of her mother clearing her throat.

"Good morning is the proper greeting. Even for someone who arrived late for breakfast."

Katherine sighed. "Good morning, Mother."

She'd barely slept, and she couldn't muster the energy it would take for a tug of war with her mother. Katherine found herself grateful that her dad was on the phone. At least she didn't have to hold a conversation with him.

Katherine smiled and thanked Diana when she placed a plate of over-medium eggs and bacon in front of her. Her mother, on the other hand, looked down at her food and frowned.

She glared at Diana. "You know I like my eggs over-easy," she scolded with venom.

Katherine blew out a frustrated breath. "Then don't order Eggs Benedict."

A woman of her breeding should know that Eggs Benedict was made with poached eggs. Yet, her mother's lack of knowledge was, of course, never her fault.

"I know what I ordered," she hissed, shoving the plate to the side. "Send it back! Tell Garland to make it the way I like it!"

Katherine shook her head and peered at the rude behavior of the elitist debutante that was her mother. The disgusting display of privilege instantly ruined her appetite. Katherine placed her fork next to the plate and slid her chair back. She was ready to flee the table when her Aunt Evelyn entered the room.

"Katie Bug!" her aunt squealed with glee, running around the table with open arms.

Katherine stood. With an open mouth, she allowed herself to be swallowed in her aunt's arms. She was truly shocked by Evelyn's presence. She hadn't seen her in a few years.

Evelyn released her and took a step back to look her up and down. "Look at you, Katie Bug! You are absolutely stunning."

"Thanks, Aunt Evelyn. You're looking great too. It's good to see you. What are you doing here?"

"Evelyn has fallen on hard times," her mother volunteered. Her tone was smug, with a hint of satisfaction, as if she was happy about her sister's misfortune. Yet, what hard times could her aunt be having? She enjoyed the same family fortune as Katherine's mom. Evelyn's inheritance ensured that she would never have to work a day in her life. She must have been running from a man. "She'll be our guest for a bit."

Under normal circumstances, a visit from her aunt would have been great. Sadly, normal was not the circumstance. Her Aunt Evelyn was a widow with a six-year-old daughter, and their home was no place for little girls.

Katherine looked past her aunt. "Where's Maddie?"

Evelyn responded with a big smile. "She's still asleep. It was a long drive from Atlanta."

"*Drive?*" Katherine questioned suspiciously.

Evelyn grinned. "I love road trips. I enjoy the scenery."

Katherine dropped down into her chair and rubbed her temples. "How long will you be staying?"

Evelyn shrugged. "I'm not sure. For a while, I guess."

Katherine looked over at her grinning dad, who was pretending to be interested in whatever business call he was on. She stared at the phone cord and imagined wrapping it around his neck until he was no more. If her mother's sour attitude hadn't spoiled her appetite, her aunt and her young cousin's presence had. The thought of a little girl in their house made Katherine sick to her stomach.

CHAPTER 6
KATHERINE

Katherine's dad pulled out a chair for Maddie and patted the seat.

"No, Maddie, come and sit by me," Katherine insisted. "I'll show you how to put on lip gloss."

Maddie giggled and skipped around the table. When she took the seat next to her, Katherine looked up at her dad and caught him glaring at her with angry eyes. She raised a brow and took her seat without a care in the world for his displeasure.

Katherine grabbed Maddie's napkin from her plate and placed it in her lap. She reached in her purse and pulled out a lip gloss with a pink tint. "How about this?" Katherine asked with a smile.

"Yes!" Maddie blurted.

Her hazel eyes sparkled with excitement as Katherine smeared the gloss on her lips. "There you go. Beautiful."

"Thanks, Katie."

"Oh, boy," Evelyn said through a breath. "She's already growing up too fast."

"Nonsense," her father interjected. "Being a lady is an art. Teach her early."

Katherine frowned and looked up at him. Her face had to have shown her abhorrence.

"You disgust me," she mouthed to her father.

He quickly looked away and turned to her mother. "I'm in the mood for the lamb. How about you?"

"I'm thinking I'll have the lobster."

"Of course, you are, darling," he chuckled, kissing her cheek.

Katherine rolled her eyes. What a display. Her parents belonged together. Her father was morally bankrupt, while her mother wore diamond blinders and pretended not to see it.

"Welcome back, Mr. and Mrs. Chase," the older waiter greeted. He turned to Katherine and nodded. "Miss Chase."

"Hello, Harrison. It's nice to see you," Katherine returned.

Cape Cod was her mother's favorite restaurant and she insisted they go out in honor of Evelyn's visit.

After greeting Evelyn and Maddie, the waiter placed menus in front of them.

"Sylvia?" a voice called from behind Harrison. Allison Crane stepped up to the table. She was wearing a tight, unflattering dress and a ton of makeup. "Fancy seeing you here."

"Allison, hello, darling. It's good to see you. Are you dining alone?"

She smiled and pointed a long nail in the direction of her husband, Jeffrey, just as he walked up with Larry, their abusive, bottom-feeding son.

"Why don't you join us?" her mother offered.

"No!" Katherine objected in a loud whisper that surely everyone heard because they all turned and glared at her. Larry narrowed his eyes as some kind of warning.

"Don't be crass," her mother scolded before turning back to the Cranes. "Please, join us."

Jeffrey pulled three chairs from a nearby table. Mr. and Mrs. Crane took a seat across the table, but Larry dragged his chair around the table to sit next to Katherine. Almost instantly, her skin heated. Her knees shook, and she was finding it difficult to breathe. Larry's close proximity to her caused a familiar reaction. She needed to get away from him.

Katherine sat her napkin down and slid back from the table. The chair made more noise than she expected, causing everyone to look at her like she was insane.

"Excuse me, please." She grabbed her purse as she stood and then hurried from the table without sharing eye contact with anyone. She'd nearly made it to the threshold to enter the hotel when someone grabbed her arm with enough aggression to stop her in her tracks. Katherine whipped around and came face to face with her mother.

"What in the hell is wrong with you?" her mother fumed. "How dare you behave like that?"

Katherine rolled her eyes and blew out a frustrated breath. "Larry attacked me, and I refuse to sit at a dinner table with him."

Her mother closed her eyes and exhaled as if she were frustrated. To make matters worse, she continued to chastise her as if she hadn't just told her that she was attacked.

"That was rude and embarrassing," she scolded.

Katherine's mouth flew open. With the same aggression, she snatched her arm away. "You are out of your fucking mind!" she seethed. "But I'm not surprised. Why would you be appalled by someone putting their hands on me? You never were before."

With tears welling in her eyes, Katherine whipped around and tore out of the restaurant.

"Get back here!" her mother gritted under her breath, no doubt trying to avoid making a scene. Appearances were everything to her mother. How she survived under her parents' roof for so long, she didn't know, but it was definitely time to go, even if she had to live on the street.

Blinded by tears, Katherine rounded a corner and ran smack into the brick wall of a man's chest. She bounced back, but the man caught her by the arms.

The voice was familiar. "Are you okay?"

Katherine dried her eyes and locked onto Joseph's hypnotic, green gaze. "Joseph," she whispered with relief.

"Are you okay?" he asked again.

Katherine held his elbows until she was steady on her feet. "Yes, I'm fine. Thank you."

He frowned. "Are you sure? Because you look like you've been crying."

Katherine wiped her face and forced a smile. "What are you doing here?" she asked, changing the subject.

"My family and I are having dinner."

Katherine was a little surprised. She's been under the impression that Joseph and his family didn't have much money. Cape Cod was fine dining at its best. It was quite an expensive restaurant.

"Would you like to join us?"

Katherine chuckled nervously. "No. Thank you. I wouldn't dream of imposing on your family dinner."

"Nonsense. It's no imposition." When he smiled, she was hit with a strange realization. Normally, Joseph's nearness sent an undeniable jolt of need to her core. Her face burned and her heart raced. Yet, she had no such reaction.

"Joseph?" she questioned, studying him through narrowed eyes.

He grinned and stretched out his hand to shake. "Jonathan. Jonathan Storm. It's nice to meet you."

Katherine ignored his hand and crossed her arms. "Not nice," she said with a frown.

Jonathan laughed. "But it was fun. Besides, you were upset. I was gonna tell you once you calmed down." He grabbed her hand and urged her along. "Come on. Let's get some dinner."

JOSEPH

Joseph raised his fork but froze before the ribeye reached his mouth, put off by the sight of Jonathan and Katherine walking hand in hand toward their table. He placed his fork on the table and glared at his brother.

For some reason, the smirk on his brother's face as they approached the table pissed him off. The glint in Jonathan's eye proved that he knew it.

"I ran into a friend of yours," he announced with delight.

For seconds, Joseph was tongue-tied. Katherine was stunning. She was wearing a tight, white dress and tall, red heels. The bottom of the dress was short and pleated, highlighting her long, shapely legs. Her long dark hair was pulled into a high ponytail, enabling her beauty to brighten the entire restaurant.

Joseph stood and found his voice. "Mom, this is Katherine Chase. We go to school together."

"It's nice to meet you, Katherine," his mother greeted with a smile. "Will you be joining us?"

"It's nice to meet you, Mrs. Storm." Katherine smiled, but Joseph could see the sadness in her beautiful, blue eyes.

"Yes. Join us," he prompted, pulling out the chair next to him.

"Okay," she acquiesced. "Thank you."

Katherine took the seat that was offered and placed her hands in her lap. She seemed anxious, but Joseph could tell it was more than that.

"Katherine, is everything okay?"

She nodded. With an appeasing smile, she responded, "Yes."

"Sooo, are you studying law as well?" his mother asked, breaking the ice.

Joseph was thankful for his mother's presence. He didn't know how to deal with her sadness. Hell, he didn't know how to handle his own emotional shit. But thanks to his mom, ten minutes later, Katherine was soon laughing, fully engaged in a conversation about her failed attempt at cooking.

Joseph sat quietly and watched as she interacted with his family. He loved to see her smile, and her laugh warmed his heart. So, when her smile faltered, he followed her line of sight across the room to Larry Crane leaving the restaurant with her father and some other people. Crane glared at them both with pure hatred.

Joseph, sensing that she was uncomfortable, covered her hand with his. "Relax, Katherine. Enjoy your dinner."

When Jonathan turned to see what they were looking at, Crane was still shooting icy daggers at them. His twin turned back to him with raised brows and a question in his eyes—Joseph's answer would determine whether Larry Crane was going to catch a beating.

Joseph shook his head, urging his brother to stand down. Crane was a weak, entitled rich boy not worth the effort it would take to ball a fist.

Joseph heard Katherine exhale as soon as Larry exited the restaurant. He didn't like her reaction to him. He didn't like anything that made her feel unsafe.

"Enjoy your dinner," Joseph repeated, giving her hand a gentle squeeze.

CHAPTER 7

KATHERINE

After waving goodbye to Joseph and his family, Katherine fished her keys out of her purse as she walked up the driveway. She had them ready by the time she reached the door. It was dark and quiet when she entered. It was after midnight, her family obviously gone to bed.

She took off her shoes and tiptoed in the dark. The last thing she wanted was to wake her parents and be forced into a conversation about her walking out on dinner. She took the stairs as quietly as possible and crept to her room, but the soft whimper of a child coming from one of the guestrooms stopped her in her tracks.

Katherine tried the doorknob, but the door was locked. She dropped to her knees and peered inside. Only, she couldn't see anything in the dark, so she stood and tiptoed back down the hall. In a cabinet at the end was where they kept a master key to all the rooms. She grabbed the key, quietly returned to the guestroom, stuck the key in the door as quietly as possible, and unlocked it.

She slowly turned the knob.

What Katherine saw when she stepped inside nearly made her heart stop.

"You son of a bitch!" she screamed.

Katherine rushed her father, snatching a lamp from the nightstand along the way, and smashed him over the head before he could jump to his feet. When he hit the floor with a yelp, she snatched her cousin from the bed and ran from the room like a bat out of hell. She carried Maddie into her bedroom and sat her down on the bed.

"You're okay," Katherine assured with a whisper. She reached for the phone on her nightstand, lifted the receiver, and dialed 911. "I need the police!"

❦

"Sorry to have wasted your time, officers," her mother said as she and her dad escorted the police to the front door.

Katherine was shocked and disgusted. No more than an hour after she called, the police were leaving without having done a thing to punish her father or protect the little girl he'd abused.

Once the door was secure, her mother whipped around, baring her fangs. "How dare you!" she hissed.

"*How dare me?*" Katherine hissed. "Are you fucking insane?" She jabbed her finger in her father's direction. "He is a monster! And so are you!"

"Get out!" her mother shouted. "I will not let you ruin this family's good name!"

Katherine glared at her mother through narrowed eyes. "So, you're okay with sleeping next to a pedophile?"

"Watch your mouth!" her father roared.

Evelyn rushed into the room and shushed them all. "Maddie is sleeping," she scolded.

Katherine looked at her aunt and shook her head. "Why wouldn't you let Maddie talk to the police?"

Evelyn blew out a harsh breath as if irritated by Katherine. "We keep family issues in the family. What were you thinking about, calling the police?"

Katherine's jaw dropped. She couldn't believe her ears. "You people are insane," she breathed.

"And you're no longer welcome in this house," her mother countered.

Katherine looked her mother in the eye. "I would rather sleep on the street than spend another night in this house. You can all go to hell!" she shouted as she ran up the stairs, finishing with, "There's a special place in hell for each of you!"

CHAPTER 8

JOSEPH

Joseph walked out of his Constitutional Law class, confident he'd passed his last final exam. Next for him was a summer internship at the prestigious law firm of Harvey and Payne, but his plan for the night was beers with his childhood friend, Jack, at their favorite watering hole.

Joseph marched down the hall with the double doors in sight, but he slowed his steps when he saw Katherine. He was hoping he'd run into her. Thoughts of her smile, her laughter, and minty scent of her shampoo kept him up all night.

Joseph walked over, planning to speak until he overheard her talking to her friend, Laverne.

"I'm in a bit of a bind," she said. "Can I stay with you for a little while?"

"Oh, damn. I'm sorry, Katie. My parents and I are going to Antigua for the summer. We leave in a couple of days."

Katherine sighed. She dropped her head and ran her fingers through her long hair. The defeated look on her face nearly broke Joseph's heart. He wanted so badly to see her smile again, and he planned to make sure that he would. Only, it wasn't the time.

He continued on without a word and pushed through the double doors.

Joseph walked out and sat on the concrete barrier, waiting patiently for Katherine to walk out. When she finally did, she looked over at him and smiled. It didn't quite reach her eyes, but at least, she was smiling.

"Hi," she greeted softly.

Joseph stood. "Hi." He could've pretended like he hadn't heard her conversation, but he wasn't the pretending kind. "I heard you need a place to stay."

Katherine quickly looked away as if embarrassed. "I... umm... I'll figure something out."

"What happened?"

She glanced at him quickly before looking away again. "Nothing. I-I gotta go."

She turned, but before she could escape, Joseph caught her by the arm. "Come and stay with me," he commanded in a soft voice.

Katherine blinked up at him, mesmerizing him with her beautiful blue eyes. "Really?"

Joseph found himself excited at the thought of sharing his space with her. "Really," he assured with a smile. "Do we need to go get your things?"

"Yes. Just a few, but... I-I don't want to put you out."

Joseph threw an arm around her and ushered her toward the parking lot. "Let's go get your things."

KATHERINE

Katherine entered the house, surprised that her parents hadn't already changed the locks. She crossed the foyer to the stairs and jogged up. Thankfully, she made it to her room without running into any of her family members.

She made quick work of gathering her things, everything she could carry. In less than ten minutes, she was trotting down the stairs, carrying two full suitcases. Just when she thought she would make it out the door, her mother and father stepped out of the parlor.

"Just what do you think you're doing?" her mother asked, crossing her arms.

"I got my things. Now, I'm going."

Her father's face twisted with anger. "Everything you own was paid for with my money. You'll leave with what's on your back."

Katherine rolled her eyes and opened the door, but her father hurried over and slammed it. He snatched the bag from her hand and tossed it to the floor.

"Get out!" he shouted, reaching for the other suitcase.

Katherine yanked it away and shoved her father backward. His eyes darkened with hatred as he advanced on her. He wrapped his fingers around her throat and forced her against the wall. She dug her fingers into his hand and struggled to pry his fingers from her throat, struggling to breathe. Just when she was getting lightheaded, salvation came in the form of a tall, muscular, green-eyed intellectual.

Joseph burst through the door and grabbed her father in a chokehold. Startled, and unable to fight, her father released her throat.

"Unhand him!" her mother screamed, running toward them.

Joseph gave her mother a look that halted her steps. He tossed her dad to the floor and hurried over to Katherine. After pulling her in his arms, he whispered, "You're okay."

He gently spoke the words that Katherine had spoken to her young cousin the day before. As Katherine struggled to catch her breath, Joseph grabbed the bag from her hand, then walked over and picked up the bag her dad had thrown to the floor.

"Let's go!" he barked. His gruff tone seemed less for her and more for her father.

Joseph waited for her to move in front of him and covered her as she made her way to the door.

"You're no daughter of mine!" her dad spat at her back.

Katherine turned around and locked eyes with her father. From the deepest part of her soul, she responded, "Robert Chase, you stopped being my father the first time you crept into my bedroom." She turned to her mother and gave her the same venom. "You are a horrible excuse for a mother. Both of you should have been sterilized before you could procreate." Katherine looked to her father. "Your money may have kept you from answering for your sins, but will it do when I go to the Tribune? Let's see if your fortune can save your good family name."

"Don't you dare threaten me!" her father bellowed.

"Fuck you!" Katherine squealed as she fled her parents' house.

Joseph's northside brownstone apartment wasn't fancy, but it was clean and nicely furnished. The decor was rustic and manly, and it smelled enticingly like Joseph. After placing her bags by the door, he gestured toward a hall.

"This way," he instructed.

Katherine followed him down the hall to a door at the end. He opened the door, ushered her inside, and flicked the light switch to reveal a small bedroom with white walls and black linen.

"You'll sleep here."

Katherine stepped inside and turned to look at Joseph. "Thank you. I really appreciate your help. I promise, I'll get a job. I won't be here too long."

Joseph shook his head and rubbed her upper arm. "Stay as long as you want." He moved to leave but stopped at the door. "The bathroom is down the hall on the right. Please make yourself at home."

He left and closed the door behind him.

Katherine walked over and placed her purse on the nightstand. She plopped down on the bed and dropped her head in her hands. Her life had spun out of control. It had never been ideal. Even though they had money, she'd had to live with a predator. She'd slept with one eye open until she turned thirteen. That was when her father had lost interest. Apparently, she'd grown too old for him.

Katherine's cheeks warmed and tears pooled in her eyes. The thought of Maddie living under her parents' roof was terrifying. She was a helpless little girl with no one, not even her mother, to protect her. Katherine swiped a tear, but more followed.

"Oh, God," she sobbed. "Please, protect Maddie."

She kicked her shoes off and lay in the fetal position on top of the cover. She knew she had to do something to protect her cousin. She just had no idea what that something was. What she did know was that every day Maddie was in that house, she was in danger.

A knock on the door startled Katherine awake. She rubbed her eyes, realizing she'd cried herself to sleep.

"Yes? Come in."

Joseph opened the door and stuck his head inside. "I made dinner if you're hungry."

Katherine sat up and smiled. "You cooked?" she asked with a raised brow.

Joseph stepped in and folded his arms. "Why do you look so surprised? I told you I could cook."

"Yeah, that's what you said," Katherine responded skeptically.

Joseph laughed. "Well, young lady, you can come see for yourself."

"Okay. I'll be out in a second."

When Joseph nodded and left the room, Katherine got up and searched her suitcase for her toiletry bag. She grabbed her toothbrush and left the room. In the bathroom, on the sink, were a set of fresh towels. After brushing, she washed her face and ran her fingers through her long, messy hair. She looked in the mirror at her red face and puffy eyes and figured she'd done all she could. It was the best she was going to look.

Katherine left the bathroom and went into the kitchen. She had to admit, whatever Joseph was cooking smelled delicious. She watched him at the stove stirring something in a pot with a towel draped over his shoulder. It certainly looked like he knew what he was doing. And she was just about to tell him that, but a knock at the door captured her attention.

Joseph turned around, surprised she'd been standing there watching him. Katherine's cheeks burned with embarrassment. She must've looked like a total creep. Thankfully, he offered a smile to put her at ease.

"Can you get that?"

"Yep." Katherine whipped around in a hurry and made her way to the door. She opened it and came face to face with a tall, handsome black man carrying two bottles of wine.

"Well, hello there," he greeted with a gleaming smile that drew a smile from Katherine.

"Hi."

When Katherine felt a hand on her back, she turned. Even though he was taller, her face was only inches from Joseph's. His nearness and the mixture of cologne and masculinity sent jolts of desire straight to her core.

Joseph pulled the door open and welcomed the man inside. "What you got there?" he asked.

"Here are the two bottles of wine I owe you," the handsome man responded.

"Oh, yeah. Come on in."

The man stepped inside and passed the wine to Joseph.

"How did your date turn out?" Joseph asked.

"It's going great," the man responded with a grin.

Joseph raised a brow. "*Going* great? You've been on a date for two days?"

The man shrugged. "And who is this beauty?"

Joseph wrapped a possessive arm around Katherine's waist. "My beauty," he responded, pulling her away from his guest.

His declaration was a shock to Katherine. But, to tell the truth, she was grinning from ear to ear on the inside.

"Katherine, this is my friend, Jack. He lives across the hall."

Katherine smiled. "It's nice to meet you, Jack."

"It's nice to meet you too, Katherine." Jack looked past Joseph. "What you got cooking over there?"

"Got a little spaghetti and fried catfish," Joseph responded with pride.

Jack grinned. "Like I taught you?"

Joseph shrugged. "For the most part."

Jack turned to Katherine. "Your guy here is being modest. He's a great cook. He learned from the best."

Joseph chuckled. "Jack, here, is a critically acclaimed personal chef. He's cooked for some very important people."

"Oh, wow. How wonderful."

"Will you and your date be joining us?" Joseph asked.

"Nah." He smirked. "I ain't ready to let her come up for air yet. Besides, I have a flight to LA tomorrow. I haven't packed." He turned to leave. "Enjoy your dinner," he said after crossing the threshold.

Joseph closed the door and turned around. His expression was concerning.

"What's wrong?" Katherine asked.

"That 'my beauty' comment. I didn't mean...well, Jack is my best friend, but he can be a bit of a flirt."

Katherine chuckled and waved off his concerns. "It's fine. I actually...well, never mind. It's fine. Can I help you in the kitchen?"

Joseph laughed with a raised brow. "I don't know. *Can* you?"

Katherine narrowed her eyes and snatched the towel from his shoulder. She swiped at him, sending him running to the kitchen. She ran behind him, swinging the cloth weapon, until he was cornered. "Just because I don't know how to cook doesn't mean I can't help. I can hand you stuff."

Joseph covered his head, feigning fear and laughed. "Okay, okay! You can help!"

"That's right, buddy, I'm useful!" Katherine proclaimed, tossing the towel at his head.

He caught the towel and tossed it back. "So violent, Miss Chase." He walked over to the table and pulled out a chair. "It just so happens, dinner is already done. Come on over here and have a seat."

Katherine took the seat he offered. She was eager to taste Joseph's cooking, but more than anything, she was starving.

CHAPTER 9
JOSEPH

After spreading the sheet on the couch, all he would need for a decent night's sleep, Joseph tossed a pillow on the couch and went into the kitchen to help Katherine with the dinner dishes.

"Joseph, really, you don't have to give up your room. I can sleep out here."

Joseph waved off her concerns and grabbed a dish towel. She washed, he dried.

"Dinner was amazing. You are quite the cook."

"Thank you."

Katherine washed and rinsed a plate but when Joseph grabbed to dry it, she held on. "I thought you worked at the Ford plant at night?"

"I do, but I took off tonight to help you get settled."

Katherine released the plate and looked up at him with furrowed brows. "Wow, I'm sorry. I have completely disrupted your life."

"Don't be silly, Katherine. Taking off is no big deal. They'll survive one night without me."

Joseph wanted to tell her that he enjoyed her presence in his home. He liked being near her.

When they finished the kitchen, Joseph grabbed a bottle of red wine from a cabinet. "Wanna glass? It's nothing fancy, but I like it."

Katherine smiled. "Yes, please," she responded politely.

Joseph pulled some glasses from a different cabinet and placed them on the table. He pulled out a chair for Katherine before searching the drawer for a corkscrew. Once he found it, he opened the bottle. While filling her glass, Joseph found himself admiring her cleavage escaping the tiny tank top she was wearing.

He looked away and slid it over.

She raised her glass and pressed it to her lips, igniting something wild in him. At that moment, he wanted nothing more than to pull her in his arms and take her right there on the table. He found himself feeling guilty about his carnal thoughts. Between the horrifying things going on in her family, and the horrifying things her father had done to her, Katherine had enough problems. She certainly didn't need to be objectified by him.

"Joseph, I meant to tell you, I really like your family. Your mom and brother seem really great. I can see the love you all have for each other."

Joseph filled his own glass and took a seat next to her. "Yes, we do love each other, but no family is perfect, Katherine. We've had our share of trials and tribulations."

"Yeah?"

Joseph dropped his head. After all, he was the main cause of said trials and tribulations.

"Yes," he admitted shamefully.

Katherine cleared her throat. "Are you done with finals?" she asked, changing the subject. Maybe she could sense how uncomfortable he was.

"Yes, I had my last final today. You?"

"One more tomorrow," she responded with a sigh of relief. "Civil Procedure."

"Then what?" Joseph asked. "Internship?"

Katherine shook her head. "It's up in the air right now. How about you?"

"I'm gonna take a leave from Ford and start my internship at Harvey and Payne."

Katherine sighed. Her expression was grim. "I was planning to intern there too."

"That's great. What's wrong?"

She shook her head and looked at him with sad eyes. "Too many ties to my dad. Too many ties to Larry Crane's family."

Joseph covered her hand with his and gave it a gentle squeeze. "Tomorrow, after your final, we'll put our heads together over a ton of alcohol and figure something out."

Katherine giggled and finished her wine. Joseph grabbed the bottle, ready to pour her a refill before she could return her glass to the table. His goal was to get her to relax and forget her family issues, if only for a little while.

"Thanks," she responded before taking a sip. "You just watch your back. Larry Crane is a vindictive bastard."

Joseph smirked at the thought of sparring with Larry Crane. No amount of money would save the spoiled rich kid if he fucked with him.

"I'll be fine, Katherine. Don't you worry about me."

Because he couldn't help himself, Joseph reached over and used his thumb to push a loose strand of hair behind her ear. In the process, his thumb brushed her soft skin. Katherine's eyes fluttered closed. A soft breath escaped her lips.

"Are you okay?" Joseph asked. "That fight you had with your folks was…"

He really didn't have the words to describe the things he'd heard. Joseph wasn't trying to stress her out. He just needed to know if she was okay.

For what seemed like hours, Katherine said nothing. In reality, it had only been about ten seconds.

"It started when I was five, maybe six. At least, that was my first recollection. Who knows, it could have started while I was in diapers."

Katherine's eyes turned red and filled with tears.

Joseph slid his chair closer and wrapped his arm around her. He could feel the tears pooling in his own eyes.

"No one will ever hurt you again."

Joseph made the promise, and it was a promise he would die to keep.

"How do you think you did?" Laverne asked, inquiring about their last final exam.

Katherine shrugged. "I got by."

Laverne grabbed her arm and turned her until they were face to face. "Are you okay?" she asked with concern.

Katherine forced a smile. "Yes, of course. I'm fine."

Laverne was a friend, but they never discussed things of significant importance. It just wasn't the nature of their relationship.

"Why did you ask if you could stay at my house?"

Katherine sighed. "It's nothing. My parents have been ragging on me lately. I needed a little space."

"Okay, I get that. So, where have you been staying?"

Katherine responded with a smile she couldn't suppress. "I'm crashing with Joseph Storm."

Laverne's mouth flew open. With wide eyes filled with questions, she asked, "Are you playing with me?"

"No. He was kind enough to let me stay with him. It's only temporary, until I get a job and find a place."

"A job?" Laverne repeated words as if Katherine had told her she was about to start turning tricks.

"Yes, a job. You're in law school. You do plan on getting one of those one day, right?"

"Yeah, but—"

"Listen, Laverne, I have to go. I have some runs to make."

Katherine gave Laverne a pacifying smile and walked away before she sounded even more like a princess. A trip down the hall and a couple of corners later, she was walking out the door. Halfway down the steps, she noticed Gabby, who appeared to be waiting for her.

"Gabby? What are you doing here?"

"Katie, I need to talk to you."

Gabby looked around as if she was making sure she wasn't being watched. Her behavior was stranger than the fact that she was actually standing on the steps of her school.

Katherine gestured for Gabby to walk with her to her car. For the entire walk to the parking lot, she looked around nervously. When they got to the car, Katherine unlocked the passenger door for Gabby then walked around and let herself in the driver's side.

"Has something happened to my parents, Gabby?"

Katherine wasted no time with small talk. She was more than curious as to why her parents' housekeeper had showed up at her school.

"No. Your parents are fine. I'm here about the girl."

Katherine's heart began to race. She trembled with fear at the thought of Maddie living under her father's roof. "What happened?" she asked, terrified of the answer.

"You know what's happening to her. Someone has to do something."

Katherine released a frustrated breath. "What can I do? I called the police. They didn't do anything. I mean... even her own mother wouldn't do a damn thing to help."

Gabby turned to her with a terrified look in her eye. "Katherine, I believe Miss Evelyn is condoning Mr. Chase's actions."

Katherine sighed. It was hard to hear, but not hard to believe. After the way her aunt had rebuffed the police and scolded her, it was painfully obvious.

"Why on earth would a mother allow a man to abuse her child?" Katherine wondered out loud.

"I'm quiet. I mind my business, but I hear everything. I overheard your aunt telling your father that her last husband took her for everything and left her in trouble with the IRS."

Katherine's mouth flew open. "How could that happen? My aunt's trust was too big to lose."

"Apparently, not. The IRS has seized her homes and frozen her accounts."

"Oh, my God."

News of Evelyn losing her fortune was unbelievable, but Katherine didn't have an ounce of sympathy for her. No amount of money should have been enough to convince someone to barter a child.

"You gotta come to the police with me," Katherine implored.

Gabby shook her head frantically. "You said, yourself, the police won't do anything. Besides, there's more. Your father has hooked up with some dangerous people, powerful people, just like him. If I get involved, your father will have me deported back to El Salvador."

Katherine frowned. "What can I do?"

"Come back home," Gabby urged. "For appearances alone, your parents will take you back."

Katherine shook her head. "I can't do that."

"You have to, Katie. There are more children involved."

Katherine's eyes grew wide. "What?" she gasped.

"Sí. More children. In your father's wine cellar, there's a secret room. There must be something in there that can help you prove he's abusing children. Something his money can't fix. Katie, you need to come home."

"No...no, I can't. I'll just sneak in while they're out or something."

Gabby dropped her head and exhaled as if defeated. "I don't know how to get into the room, and your father changed all the locks in the house. If he knows you can't get in, he'll accuse me or someone else from the staff. It'll take time to find the keys."

Katherine pushed her hair behind her ear and placed her hand over Gabby's.

"I've been *interrupting* your father every chance I get. I don't know how much longer I'll be able to do that."

"I'll figure something out. Something that doesn't involve me moving back into that house. Please, do your best to look out for Maddie."

"Okay," Gabby relented with a sigh. "I'll do my best. Please, don't take too long."

Gabby climbed out of the car and disappeared around a van. Katherine started the car and did her best to force away the image of her innocent little cousin, her dad, secret rooms, and powerful predators.

A quick trip to the supermarket and a short drive later, Katherine was ringing the bell to Joseph's apartment. Seconds later, he hopped down the stairs and opened the door. He grabbed the grocery bags from her hand and propped the door open with his body.

"Hey. How'd you do on your final?" he asked as she entered.

"I'm pretty sure I did fine. How was your day?"

"Fine. Got some household things done."

They entered the apartment, which was spotless, and the smell of cleaning products was in the air. "You've been busy," Katherine commented.

"Yes, I have. With school and work, I have very little time to get things done. Thought I'd take advantage of my day off. By the way, I had keys made for you. They're on the table." Joseph entered the kitchen and put the bags on the counter. "What's all this?" he asked.

"Oh, I just picked up a few things. I thought I'd fix you lunch for work tonight."

Joseph turned around with a grin. "You're gonna make my lunch? As in cooking?"

"No," Katherine chuckled. "More like slapping cold cuts on bread."

"Whew! Thank God," he joshed with laughter.

Katherine glared at him through narrowed eyes. "Oh, hush!"

She walked over and helped him put the groceries away.

"Relax. I got this. We both know you're not accustomed to domestic labor," Joseph teased. "Go on over there and have a seat."

He was joking, but he wasn't lying. Katherine had grown up with a household staff. She didn't cook or clean, and she didn't have the first clue how to do laundry. She'd even felt a bit out of sorts at the supermarket as she hadn't done any of the household shopping. Thankfully, her dad hadn't canceled her credit cards because, without them, she didn't have any money.

Katherine sighed, walked over to the couch, and plopped down, disgusted with the fact that she was a grown woman with no idea how to take care of herself.

"Do you have any plans for Memorial Day weekend?" Joseph asked from the kitchen.

"Huh?" Memorial Day had completely slipped her mind. Normally, her family would have a pretentious barbecue at their home. It was never a fun, relaxed event with delicious, messy food or drinks and laughter shared by friends and family. It was the type of event where men showed up with jackets, women wore heels, and insignificant people made business deals. She never got excited about holidays.

"No."

Joseph left the kitchen and walked into the living room. "You're welcome to hang with me at my mom's. We're gonna have a barbecue."

"Okay. Yeah, thanks."

Katherine looked up at Joseph and wondered what she'd done to deserve such a thoughtful friend.

Friend?

Were they friends? If not, what were they? And what did she have to lose by asking?

"Are we friends, Joseph?"

Joseph sat next to her and relaxed against the cushion. "For now," he said with a sexy, crooked grin. "But can I be honest?"

"Of course."

"I'm afraid to show you my true feelings."

Katherine frowned. "Why?"

Joseph sighed. He sat up and clutched Katherine's hand. "It's your father," he admitted. "He used his authority as your father to heinously abuse you for years. To be honest, I'm afraid to push. I'm afraid to touch you. I don't want you to feel like I'm taking advantage of you, Katherine. I want you to feel safe with me."

With tears in her eyes, Katherine smiled and caressed his chiseled jaw. "I feel safe with you, Joseph. The safest I've ever felt."

She moved close until their lips were a breath apart. Before he could retract, Katherine pushed her lips to his. As she kissed him, she prayed he reciprocated. When he did, she inhaled with relief and pushed her fingers through his thick hair. When his lips parted and he offered his tongue, Katherine melted with desire. Joseph cupped her face and deepened the kiss, drawing a moan from the deepest part of her. She was shocked with jolt after jolt of desire that traveled directly to her wet center. But sadly, he pulled away. It was like someone had doused ice water on her.

Katherine's eyes blinked open. She stared at him with desperation, wondering what she had done wrong.

"Joseph?" she croaked, her voice hoarse and filled with desire.

He released her face and turned to the TV. Katherine followed his line of sight. What could have happened to make him turn so quickly?

The news was on.

A female newscaster was reporting on a plane crash.

· · ·

"FLIGHT 191, CARRYING 277 PASSENGERS FROM CHICAGO O'Hare Airport to Los Angeles, has crashed. The plane, loaded with fuel, exploded on impact. Sadly, there were no survivors."

"JACK WAS ON THAT PLANE," HE SAID IN A SAD WHISPER.

CHAPTER 11
JOSEPH

"I've never been on this side of town," Katherine admitted.

Joseph wasn't surprised. They were in Bronzeville, a community comprised of prominent Blacks. Though Katherine wanted to practice law dealing with Immigration and Civil Rights issues, because of her stuffy and privileged upbringing, she hadn't had much experience with neither blacks nor immigrants. But Joseph wasn't judging. He understood that he also fell into the category of privileged. He was a white, Anglo-Saxon male. Not too many in America were more privileged than he and his twin brother.

He didn't want to offend her, but he had to ask. "Have you ever really been around black people?"

Katherine shrugged and dropped her head with shame. "Only the really rich ones," she admitted. "Oh, and Vera Campbell from school. We've studied together a few times. But, other than Laverne, I mostly keep to myself."

Joseph understood. Katherine had been through a lot. She was abused and betrayed by the person... no, people she should have been able to trust the most. Getting close to others couldn't have been easy.

He could relate. He didn't get close to many, mostly because he didn't want others to discover his shameful secret.

Joseph pulled to the curb and parked in front of the house where Jack had grown up. He walked around and opened the door for Katherine. After helping her out, he grabbed the fruit tray and Bundt cake she'd insisted they buy. According to his little debutante, showing up at the house of a bereaving family empty handed was a no-no.

Katherine looked up at the Grant's home as they walked up the pathway. "How lovely," she marveled.

"Yes, this area, even though it was meant to keep blacks in racial bubble, strived with the help of successful black professionals. Jack's parents own funeral homes. Six, to be exact. They're very successful."

"That's wonderful. I feel so bad, Joseph. Jack seemed like a very nice man."

Joseph sighed. "He was the best." He handed her the cake. The Grants didn't know her, and he thought she'd feel more comfortable if she walked in with something to offer. After all, the cake and fruit tray were her idea. He placed his hand at the small of her back. For a brief moment, he recalled the kiss they'd shared. It was like no other kiss he'd ever had. He'd never felt the same for any other woman. Joseph wanted to devour her. He wanted touch every part of her, inside and out.

"Joseph, hi!" Jack's mother greeted from the porch.

She must have seen them walking up. Joseph walked up the steps and wrapped his free arm around Jack's mother. "I'm so sorry, Mrs. Grant. You know if there is anything you need me to do, I'm here."

Jack's mom wrapped her arms around Joseph and gave him a tight squeeze. "I know that, son."

For minutes, she held him. Through her embrace, Joseph felt her pain. Brenda Grant was a loving mother. She had five children and managed to show all of them an abundance of love and affection.

When she finally released him, she looked up and asked, "How's your mother?"

"She's fine. She's on her way," Joseph told the older woman.

"She is?" Katherine inquired.

Joseph turned and noted the surprised look on her face.

"She's an angel," Mrs. Grant interjected. "And who is this beauty, Joseph?"

Joseph slipped his arm around Katherine's waist. He knew it was a possessive gesture, but he was fine with it. Mrs. Grant had been telling him he needed a good woman for years. "This is Katherine Chase."

Brenda Grant smiled and squeezed Katherine's shoulder. "It's nice to meet you, Katherine Chase."

Katherine smiled and handed her the cake. "It's nice to meet you, Mrs. Grant. It's not much, but we brought a Bundt cake. I'm so sorry for your loss."

Mrs. Grant's eyes darkened with sadness. "Thank you, dear. And thanks for this. We could use something sweet in here."

Joseph looked over at Katherine with a smile. He was thankful he'd listened to her about the cake and fruit tray. No one really knew what to do when visiting someone who'd lost their loved one. But she'd been right, and he was grateful they hadn't shown up empty-handed. At the very least, whatever was brought would provide something to talk about, ease a bit of the awkward silence.

"Well, come on in." Mrs. Grant pulled the screen door open and held it for them to enter.

Joseph stepped into the foyer and admired the marble floors and chic abstract paintings on the walls. On a circular glass table sat a crystal vase with fresh cut lilies inside.

"This new?" Joseph asked, pointing to the painting.

"Yes, Alicia got it for us on her last trip to Paris."

Alicia, her daughter, was an art conservator.

Mrs. Grant led them into the living room where the rest of her family had gathered. "Joseph's here," she announced.

"Hey," he greeted with a wave.

The family returned his greeting with smiles.

"This is Miss Katherine Chase. Joseph's lady."

"Hello," Katherine greeted. "My condolences to you all."

"Thank you," a few responded.

Alicia, Jack's sister, stood from the couch and walked over to Katherine. "Hi. I'm Alicia." She looked down at the cake. "And, what's this?"

"Oh, yeah..." Katherine handed her the cake. "It's a Bundt cake."

"Thank you, Katherine. Would you like something to eat?"

Katherine smiled. "I could eat."

"Make yourself at home. I'll fix you a plate."

"Thank you," Katherine responded.

"Joey, how 'bout you? You hungry?"

Mrs. Grant laughed. "When is he not? Girl, go in there and fix him a plate."

Alicia chuckled and disappeared into the kitchen. Joseph walked into the connecting dining room and pulled a chair out for Katherine. When she sat, he took a seat next to her.

"Joey?" she questioned with a raised brow. "I didn't know you went by Joey."

"I don't," Joseph grumbled.

Katherine chuckled. "Well, you better go in there tell Alicia."

Joseph chucked his thumb toward the kitchen. "She just likes to get under my skin."

"She's very pretty. I sense some history."

"Nah. Well... I had a crush her a while back."

Katherine studied him with furrowed brows. "And?"

"And nothing. Jack threatened to cut off my balls if I touched his sister. Besides, she wasn't into me."

Katherine grinned. "That's not the vibe I got."

Joseph leaned closer to her and spoke into her ear. "Are you jealous, Miss Chase?"

"Of course not, Joey," she rebutted with a cheeky grin.

"Cute. Very cute. Anyway, I've known the Grants for years. Jack and I were in the fourth grade together."

Katherine looked up at him with sympathetic eyes and whispered, "Oh, wow. I'm so sorry, Joseph."

Joseph nodded and caressed her hand. "Thank you."

KATHERINE

Joseph unlocked the door and stepped to the side. He was quiet on the way home and so was Katherine. She wanted to comfort him, but she didn't have the words. Their visit with Grants had started out solemn but calm, until Jack's grandmother arrived. Mrs. Grant and her children had tried to console her, but she was inconsolable. The older woman collapsed in her son's arms and wailed painfully.

In the presence of such sadness, Katherine hadn't been able to hold back the tears. Joseph's mom had rubbed his back as his eyes filled with moisture. He was obviously uncomfortable with public displays of sadness, so Mrs. Storm had suggested Katherine take him home. And, of course, Joseph didn't argue.

"Would you like a glass of wine?" Katherine asked. She figured since he'd taken off from work again, he could have a drink.

Joseph went into the living room and sat on the couch. "I'll take a beer."

"Okay." Katherine grabbed a beer out of the refrigerator and sat next to him. "Do you need anything else?"

He threw his arm over her shoulder and pulled her close. "Thanks for riding with me. Mrs. Grant said that you were sweet."

Katherine smiled and handed him the beer. "Sweet, huh?"

"Yeah. I think you're sweet too. I like you being here, Katherine."

She giggled. "Even though you had to give up your room?"

Joseph nodded. "Even though," he confirmed.

The shrill ring of the telephone tore through the silence. Joseph lifted the beer to his lips and took a sip. "Do you mind grabbing that?"

"Sure." Katherine got up, walked into the kitchen, and grabbed the receiver from the wall mount. "Hello?"

For a few seconds, the caller was silent.

"Hello?" she called again.

"H-hello. Is Joseph there?" The caller was a woman.

Katherine ignored the sting of jealousy and covered the receiver. She waved the phone toward Joseph. "It's a woman."

Joseph shrugged. "What woman?"

Katherine frowned, but she was staying there rent-free. The least she could do was play secretary. "May I please ask who's calling?"

"Who is this?" the caller asked with a boatload of attitude.

"May I please ask who's calling?" Katherine repeated.

"This is Cynthia Nichols, and I'd like to speak with Joe Storm."

Katherine rolled her eyes. She knew Cynthia. They weren't friends. In fact, Cynthia didn't have many friends. She was very pretty but wasn't the nicest woman at their school.

"Please, hold," Katherine said in a dry tone.

She placed the receiver on the counter and walked over to the couch and sat down. "It's Cynthia Nichols."

Joseph seemed surprised. He placed his beer on the cocktail table and stood. Katherine stared at his muscular back as he walked over to the phone.

He picked up the receiver. "Hello?" After a few seconds, he asked, "How did you get my number?"

Cynthia must've asked him who the woman was that answered the phone because his next words were, "Oh, yeah. That was my girl-friend... Yes, Cynthia. I have a girlfriend."

Joseph returned the receiver and walked back over to the couch. It hadn't escaped Katherine that he had claimed for the second time in a few days. Even though it was just smoke and mirrors, it felt good to hear.

Joseph grabbed his beer from the table, finished it off, then took the bottle in the kitchen and tossed it in the trash. After grabbing another from the fridge, he said, "I'm gonna grab a shower," before disappearing down the hall.

Katherine got up and went into the kitchen. She grabbed the day's paper and tossed it onto the kitchen table, then she grabbed a glass from the cabinet and helped herself to Joseph's wine. After filling her glass, she sat at the table and poured through the want ads. She couldn't live off Joseph forever. She needed a job as soon as possible.

For twenty minutes, she perused the want ads, circling jobs she wasn't qualified for. She had never had a job in her life, never needed one. Even though her dad pretended to be a businessman, no one in their family actually worked. Because of generational wealth, they'd never had to.

Katherine finished her wine and washed the glass out in the sink. She was heading to bed with no prospect of employment.

It was quiet when she passed the bathroom—Joseph must've been done with his shower.

With the intention of getting ready for bed, Katherine opened the door and got a delicious eyeful of Joseph's wet, naked body wrapped only in a towel. His dark hair was still damp, and water drizzled down his chiseled chest and abs.

Katherine inhaled a sharp breath and froze. Her eyes must've been bulging out of her head. In her entire life, she'd never seen anything more beautiful.

"I-I'm sorry," she apologized with a gasp.

Joseph looked over at her with knitted brows. He seemed concerned but completely comfortable, which was a bit backward since he was the one naked.

"No, Katherine. *I'm* sorry. I just came in here to grab some pajamas. I thought I could get in and out before you came in."

Katherine tore her eyes from his exquisite form and forced herself to look directly into his eyes. "It's okay. I'm invading your space. I don't want to make you feel uncomfortable in your own home."

In two strides, Joseph was close enough for her to smell the mint on his breath and the shampoo in his hair. Katherine's skin tingled and butterflies danced in her stomach.

Joseph cupped her face. "Don't say that, Katherine. You're not invading my space, and I feel very comfortable. Do you believe me?"

His scent, wafting in the air around her, drove her crazy.

Joseph gave her a questioning glare. When she acknowledged with a nod, he gave her a gentle kiss on the forehead.

"Goodnight, Katherine," he said as he left the room.

CHAPTER 12

KATHERINE

Katherine crept down the pathway that ran along the side of her parents' house. She'd been in constant contact with Gabby over the past few weeks. Then, finally, Gabby had called to tell her that she'd found the key to the secret room in his wine cellar. She'd said her parents were attending a charity ball and her aunt was on a date. It was the perfect time to see what her father was really up to.

"Hurry!" Gabby shouted in a whisper from the doorway.

Katherine hurried inside through the back door. She followed Gabby through the house, down to the wine cellar, to a wall with wood paneling. She pushed on of the panels and a small section of the wall popped out.

Gabby slid it open. "In here," she whispered.

Gabby turned on a flashlight and stepped into the dark room.

Katherine walked over and stood in front of the door, terrified. Not of the boogeyman or some monster attacking her in the dark. She was afraid of seeing the proof of her father's sins.

She heard a click when Gabby pulled on a thin chain hanging from the ceiling, and then there was light. When her eyes adjusted to the change, she looked around the room. Except for a couple of file cabinets, a desk, and a box, there wasn't much.

"Over here," Gabby whispered as she hurried to the file cabinet.

Gabby opened it and pulled out one of the files. Katherine could see the terror in her eyes as she handed it over. The word, "Playhouses" was written on the outside of the folder. Katherine opened the folder with shaky hands and looked at the papers, which were a six-page list of names and addresses. Next to each name was either "girl" or "boy" written inside parentheses. Katherine could hope and pray that what she was reading didn't mean what she thought it meant, but it would be no use.

Katherine and Gabby looked through a few more files, but they wouldn't have time to sift through them all. Gabby put the files back, and they moved to the desk. After rummaging through a few drawers, they didn't find anything other than a few office supplies.

They made sure to return everything the way they found it and moved on to the box. Katherine lowered to a squat, lifted the lid, and instantly regretted it. What she found inside was the property of a person with a special place in hell waiting for them. In fact, her father may very well be the devil himself.

JOSEPH

The sound of the lock turning gave Joseph a feeling of excitement. He hurried over to the stove and checked on his Coq au vin. It was the only French dish Jack had taught him to make. Since Katherine had once told him she loved French cuisine, preparing the French chicken dish was both a tribute to his friend and a way of pampering Katherine.

She entered the apartment and sat her purse on a table by the door. "Hey," she greeted.

"Hey, yourself." Joseph walked over to her and lifted her face for a kiss, but her uneasy demeanor gave him pause. "What's wrong?"

With her eyes filled with tears, Katherine shook her head. "Nothing. It's nothing."

She turned to escape but Joseph caught her arm. "Don't do that, Katherine. Talk to me."

She swiped a tear from her cheek and looked up at him with sad eyes. It was at that moment that Joseph realized what he wanted most was for Katherine to be happy, and he would be the one to ensure her happiness.

"Come here. Sit," he told her, leading her to the sofa.

Joseph sat, pulling her down with him. "Tell me," he insisted, massaging her shoulder.

Katherine was shaking. She closed her eyes and inhaled a deep breath. Once she got herself together, she opened her eyes and gave him the rundown of her day. Hearing about her father and his network of monsters made him nauseous.

"I have to do something," she breathed, with desperation in her tone.

It almost seemed like she felt somehow responsible for her father's actions. When Joseph looked into her eyes, he swore he saw guilt.

"Why do you have to do something? I want you to stay away from him. Call the police. Let them handle it."

Katherine exhaled her frustration. "I've called the police. He's either paying them off, or they just don't care. As long as it doesn't interfere with their lavish lifestyles, my mother and my aunt don't care. Poor Gabby hasn't slept in weeks, trying to keep my little cousin safe. If I don't do something, who will?"

Joseph shook his head. There had to be another way to expose her father and his tribe of maggots that didn't involve Katherine putting herself at risk. "What can you do?"

"I might know someone who can help. I'm gonna give him a call tomorrow."

Joseph frowned. "Him? Who's him?"

"His name is Rick Bolin. He's a friend. He works for the FBI."

He didn't like the sound of that, but Katherine was determined, and Joseph understood. Of course, she wanted to help, but trying to bring down a network of criminals was working too close to the fire. Though, one thing was for certain. He wasn't about to let her burn.

❧❦❧

Joseph unlocked the door and opened it for Katherine to enter. He stepped inside the small diner behind her and looked around for her friend.

"There he is," she said, waving to a man in the corner.

Her friend stood and waved as they approached. Joseph could see how Rick Bolin would be good-looking to women. With an overly wide grin, he looked Katherine up and down. He was tall and fit with blond hair and blue eyes, like a California surfer.

He opened his arms for a hug. With a clenched jaw, Joseph intercepted, sticking his hand out.

"Joe Storm," he introduced. "You must be Rick?"

Rick's smile fell. Joseph could see the debate in his eyes when he looked down at his hand, but Joseph stood his ground. The Fed would have to be content with a handshake because he wasn't about to get a hug.

"Nice to meet you, Joe," Rick relented, shaking Joseph's hand. He looked over at Katherine. "Hey, Katie. It's good to see you again."

She smiled. "Rick, hi. How've you been?"

"Can't complain." He gestured toward the booth. "Have a seat."

Katherine took a seat opposite Rick, and Joseph slid in beside her. Rick slid inside the booth with his eyes trained on Joseph.

Joseph smiled. "Thanks for meeting *us*."

He made sure to emphasize the "us" to her friend.

"No problem. If what you're telling me is true—"

"It's true," Katherine interjected. "I've seen the proof. There are files with names and addresses. There are polaroid pictures of children, some with..." She trailed off, unable to finish the sentence. "You've gotta do something."

"I will, but you'll have to go on record. I have to sign you up as a confidential informant. I can't get a search warrant without it. Are you willing to do that?"

"Yes, I am. I'll do whatever you need."

Joseph frowned and turned to Katherine. "You know your father, but you don't know these other men. You could be putting yourself in danger."

"I don't care, Joseph," she huffed.

"I care!" Joseph barked, a little louder than he'd intended.

Katherine grabbed his hand under the table and looked him in the eyes. "Joseph, we're talking about children. There were even babies in the pictures."

She dropped her head in her hand and began to sob. Joseph wrapped his arm around her and pulled her close. As she cried into his chest, he realized that Katherine was all in. There was nothing he could do or say to stop her from getting waist deep in a very dangerous situation.

"I'm sorry, sweetheart," Joseph whispered in her ear.

Of course, her involvement in taking down a child sex ring, ran by her father, was important to her. Because of everything she'd been through, it was personal.

Rick reached across the table and touched her arm. "Katie, I'll have a search warrant by tomorrow. We're gonna bury those bastards," he promised.

Joseph found himself praying that Rick could make good on his promise. He wanted nothing more than for Katherine to exorcise every demon from her childhood, and he would do whatever it took to help her.

CHAPTER 13
KATHERINE

Joseph opened the door. "Go get prettied up. We're going out."

Katherine entered the apartment, tossed her purse on the table, and turned to Joseph, a hand on her hip. "Going out?" she asked with a raised brow. "Out where?"

"We're done with finals. You're about to put a nail in your dad's coffin. It's time for a little fun."

Joseph locked the door and walked to the living room. He turned on the TV and plopped down on the couch. "Is it gonna take you long to get ready?"

"Get ready for what?" Katherine asked.

"Dinner, first. Then, dancing and drinks."

Katherine laughed. "You dance?"

"No," Joseph scoffed. "I'm gonna drink. You're gonna dance."

"Figures," Katherine muttered.

"Go."

"All right, all right." Katherine giggled and hurried to the bedroom. Joseph was right. She'd worked hard all semester and Rick was on the road to take down her father. It was definitely time for a little fun.

It only took Katherine a half hour to get dressed, but you would think it took hours the way Joseph stared at her.

"What?" Katherine exclaimed. "I didn't take that long."

"No, sweetheart, but it wouldn't take long for you. You go to bed and wake up gorgeous."

Katherine smiled. She'd worn the tiny red dress she picked, hoping it would make Joseph a little less gentleman-like. Her cheeks warmed. So, she knew she was blushing.

"Thank you," was her shy response, leaving her feeling awkward.

Joseph was ridiculously sexy in blue jeans and a fitted black shirt. Like the sun, it was dangerous to look directly at him. Had she had more courage, she would have run to him, tore the shirt from his body, and begged him to make her a woman. A complete woman.

"Joseph, you look *so* good."

"Yeah?" He grinned and moved closer. "You think so?"

Katherine nodded. "Yeah, I do."

He slipped an arm around her waist and pulled her to his hard body. He lifted her chin with a finger and pressed his lips to hers. Katherine exhaled and melted against him.

He broke the kiss and gazed at her through hooded eyelids. "I wanna take you to bed," he rasped.

Joseph's hand slid slowly down her back to cup her ass. Katherine could feel his hardness pressed against her stomach, and the smirk he brandished hinted that he knew she could feel it.

He took a step back and gripped the large bulge in his jeans. The very sight of him had Katherine's panties clinging to her wetness.

"For now, we'll start with dinner," he said with a mischievous grin.

JOSEPH

Watching Katherine bounce around the dance floor to Rod Stewart's "If You Want My Body" made Joseph smile. Her family life seemed to have been filled with abuse and isolation, so it made him happy to see her enjoying herself. Not to mention, she looked like a goddess in the tiny red dress that hugged her womanly curves.

"Can I get you anything else?" a waitress shouted over the music.

With hesitation, Joseph diverted his attention from Katherine to the woman standing over him.

"Anything at all?" she inquired with a raised brow and lustful gaze.

Joseph smiled. "Yes. You can get me another beer and a glass of red wine for my lady."

With a newly sour expression, the waitress nodded and walked away.

Joseph returned his attention to Katherine to find her dancing with a man in a loud, shiny suit. Not wanting to ruin her fun, he had no intention of interrupting. They were just dancing, and dancing was harmless. Still, he watched the man like a hawk to make sure it remained harmless. And it did until the man in the greasy suit slipped an arm around Katherine's waist. It must have made her feel uneasy because she stopped dancing and stepped out of his grasp.

Joseph was already on his feet when the man reached for her again. When Katherine slapped the man's hand away, he brandished a smirk and moved to close the distance between them. Joseph covered her with an arm and guided her out of the man's reach. He had to look down to stand nose to nose with the shorter man.

"You got some kind of fucking problem?"

The man grinned. "No, man. I got no problems," he responded with a condescending chuckle.

"You're about to," Joseph warned, staring the man down.

The man in the pimp suit threw his hands up in surrender and slithered away.

Joseph turned to Katherine. "You okay?"

"Yep," she answered with a smile. She slid her arms around his neck and pushed her body against his. "He got you on the dance floor."

Joseph laughed and shook his head. "Oh, no, lady. I told you, I don't dance."

Katherine locked him in her grasp and swiveled her hips. Joseph relented. He held her around the waist and humored her with a two-step. Maybe it was because she was in his arms, but he wasn't as put off by dancing as much as he thought he'd be.

Katherine's dark hair bounced around her face as she danced. She seemed light, carefree, and at peace, which gave him a feeling of peace.

"I thought I'd never see the day," said a familiar voice.

Joseph stopped dancing and turned, coming face to face with Nate who was grinning from ear to ear with Cynthia Nichols tucked under his arm. Cynthia, however, was not smiling. If looks could kill, Joseph couldn't tell if her hateful glare was deadlier for him or Katherine.

"What's up, Joe?" Without waiting for a response, Nate's eyes skipped over to Katherine. "Hey, Katie. Fancy meeting you here."

"Hey, Nate. It's good to see you," she greeted cheerfully. "Cynthia, hi."

"Katherine," Cynthia dryly acknowledged.

Joseph looked over just as the waitress placed their drinks on the table. "Drinks have arrived," he announced.

With his hand pressed to the small of Katherine's back, Joseph ushered her toward the table.

"We'll join you!" Nate shouted over the music.

Joseph didn't mind his company; Nate was a friend. Cynthia, on the other hand, was in a foul mood, obviously brought on by jealousy.

"I didn't know you two were a thing," she remarked accusingly.

Joseph pulled out Katherine's chair then waved toward them. "I didn't know you two were a thing," he threw back at her, causing her to quickly look away.

After all, she had just recently called him, no doubt with a proposition.

Joseph took a seat next to Katherine and handed her the glass of wine. She had a smirk on her face, and he suspected she was amused by his and Cynthia's exchange. He gave her a winked and grabbed his beer.

"Look what I got," Nate blurted, totally oblivious to the irony of the conversation around him. He pulled out a plastic bag of pot and tossed it on the table. "I got the good shit, my friend."

Nate was a brilliant law student, but a stoner for sure. On occasion, Joseph would take a hit, but Nate woke up and went to bed with a joint in his mouth. He looked over at Katherine, and he couldn't begin to imagine her getting stoned.

"You partake?" Joseph asked her.

Katherine shrugged. "Every blue moon, but I'm game. Roll it up."

"Already done," Nate crowed, waving a joint around.

"Should we go outside?" Cynthia suggested.

"Nah," Nate said, dismissing the suggestion. "I smoke in here all the time. With all the smoke in here, they'll never know who's burning grass."

He put the joint to his lips and lit it. After a few puffs, he inhaled deep and passed it to Katherine. Cynthia seemed offended by the slight and rolled her eyes. Katherine took a couple of hits and handed it to Joseph. He followed suit and handed it to Cynthia.

"Well, thank you," she scoffed.

The joint went around twice until there was nothing left. Joseph looked over to check on Katherine—she was sipping her wine and appeared to be perfectly fine—but when Abba's "Dancing Queen" blared through speakers, she grabbed Joseph's hand.

"Come on!" she shouted, pulling him out of his seat and toward the dance floor.

Katherine was successful in getting him to his feet, but there was no way she was getting him back on the dance floor.

He yanked her close to his body and whispered in her ear, "I came, I danced, I'm done. I'm not going back out there, doll."

"Take Cynthia with you," Nate suggested, pulling Cynthia out of her seat before Katherine could protest.

Joseph could tell by their expressions that neither one of them wanted to dance with each other. Nevertheless, they made their way to the dance floor.

"So, you're the man that got the woman," Nate remarked.

Joseph looked over at his friend. "What does that mean?"

"Man, you gotta know Katherine is the ultimate prize. She's super smart, drop-dead gorgeous, and she comes from a good family."

Good family? If he only knew.

"She's not a prize." Joseph found himself irritated. "She's an intelligent woman who's more than what she looks like. For a fact, she's more than her overprivileged, tainted family."

"Okay, bro. I hear you. I don't know her like that, but I'm sure you're right. I'm just happy your cranky ass has a woman in your life."

Joseph frowned. "Cranky?"

"Yeah, dude, cranky," Nate doubled down. "All you do is work and go to school. Have a little fun."

"I was having fun until you showed up."

Nate shrugged. "Yeah, but I brought the good grass."

Joseph laughed. "That you did."

Nate sat back in his seat and turned serious. "Hey, Joe. I'm really sorry about Jack. I know that was your guy."

Joseph sighed. "Thanks," he said, turning his attention to Katherine. She was dancing, but not with the same vigor as before. She, clearly, wasn't having as good a time as before. Maybe Cynthia's presence was bringing her down.

"We're gonna get outta here," Joseph said to Nate.

Standing, he pulled some cash from his pocket, dropped a couple of bills on the table, and looked back at Nate. "Pay the tab." He then walked over to the dance floor and cupped Katherine's elbow. "Ready to go home?"

The look of relief in her eyes was all the confirmation he needed.

She nodded and followed him off the dance floor.

Nate waved, lighting another joint as they walked by.

KATHERINE

When Joseph opened the door, Katherine kicked off her shoes and took off running to the bathroom. At dinner, she'd had two glasses of wine, and she'd had two more at the disco. Maybe it was because she was stoned, but everything Joseph had said during the ride home made her laugh. Stoned or not, four glasses of wine and laughter could surely test a bladder.

She hurried inside the bathroom and closed the door. After a lengthy pee, Katherine flushed and washed her hands. She left the bathroom and joined Joseph in the kitchen where was putting their leftovers from dinner in the fridge. He turned around when Katherine cleared her throat. "What?" he asked.

"I wanna warm that food up," she admitted with a grin.

"You're really hungry?"

Katherine shrugged. "I could eat."

She wasn't surprised by Joseph's puzzled expression since it hadn't been too long since they'd had dinner.

"You got the munchies," he accused with laughter.

She giggled. "Maybe."

He smiled and pulled the leftovers out of the fridge. "Go on over there and relax. I'll pop these leftovers in the oven."

Katherine took the bag of food from his hand. "No worries. I'll eat it cold."

Joseph chuckled and closed the refrigerator. "Okay, lady."

Katherine took the bag into the living room, turned on the TV, and changed the channel until she happened upon *The Benny Hill Show*. She sat on the floor with her back against the cocktail table and pulled the Styrofoam tray out of the bag. The delicious aroma of her pork chop escaped when she opened the tray.

"Mmmm."

With nary a knife or fork, she dug in, picking up the pork chop and taking a huge bite. But she nearly choked, laughing at the crazy antics of Benny Hill.

"Whoaaaa! Slow down, hungry lady," Joseph said as he entered the room, carrying two glasses of wine. He took a seat on the floor next to her and shook his head. "I can't believe you're eating cold pork chops."

Katherine grinned. "Not cold, room temperature," she corrected before taking another bite.

Joseph handed her a glass of wine and looked up at the television. "I can't believe you're watching Benny Hill."

Katherine giggled again. "It's late. What else is on?"

When she giggled a third time, she realized she'd been giggling a lot. After another bite of the delicious, lukewarm chop, she took a sip and washed it down with wine.

Joseph, amused, looked over at her with the sexiest smirk. "You're having the time of your life, aren't you?"

"A ball," Katherine admitted. She was in a great place. She had a nice, thick pork chop, an almost full glass of wine, and the man of her dreams sitting beside her.

She crossed her legs and took another bite.

At least, for that moment, she was at peace.

CHAPTER 14

"Katherine." After a few nudges, Katherine realized Joseph was calling her name. She must've fallen asleep on the floor. When she opened her eyes, he was leaning over her, running his thumb along her hairline.

"We fell asleep," he whispered.

Joseph's face was close enough for her to see the golden specks of hazel in his minty green eyes. Katherine's eyes lowered to his soft lips. She imagined them blanketing her skin with sensual kisses.

She reached up and her fingers along the five o'clock shadow covering chiseled jaw. She gazed into his eyes, hoping he could see the desire burning from within.

"*Katherine.*" His whisper was a warning. A warning Katherine could not take heed.

She pulled his face to hers and took his lips. Joseph wrapped his arm around her and held her tight to his body. His kiss grew feverish, proving he wanted her too.

Katherine embraced him and pulled him on top of her. "I need you, Joseph," she whispered against his lips.

Joseph pulled back and looked her in the eye. "Are you sure?"

"Yes, Joseph. Please." She heard the desperation in her voice.

Joseph looked at her through hooded lids while running his hand slowly up her inner thigh. He lowered to the crook of her neck and kissed along her collarbone. His tongue warmed her skin, sending bolts of fire directly to her center.

"Joseph," she breathed, wanting more.

"I'm here," he whispered near her ear.

Joseph's hand crawled up her thigh until he reached her panties. Katherine drew a sharp breath as he massaged her covered pussy. He took her lips and kissed her with a passion that had her squirming beneath him, but when he suddenly stopped and rose to his knees, she was left feeling cold.

Her eyes flew open. She looked up at him, wondering if she'd done something wrong, until she looked into his eyes and saw desire.

"Joseph?"

With a devilish grin, Joseph reached down and undid the side-zipper on her dress. He slipped a hand behind her and lifted her back from the floor. Katherine raised her arms and wiggled to aid him in removing her dress. Next, was her bra.

"Beautiful," he said as he placed it on the floor beside her.

He lowered until their lips touched. Katherine's lips parted instinctively, allowing his tongue to explore. Joseph evoked a moan when he lowered her to the floor and deepened the kiss.

Katherine reached to wrap her arms around his neck, but Joseph caught her hands and pinned them above her head. Just as she'd fantasized, he warmed her skin with tender kisses, cupped her breasts and kissed the space between them. He kissed his way over to her breast. Cool air tickled her nipple when he licked it. "

So beautiful," he whispered before sucking it into his warm mouth.

Katherine gasped and cupped the back of his head. She had never felt anything so exquisite in her life. For the first time, she wasn't cringing at the thought of being touched. She wanted his hands everywhere.

Joseph kissed a line down her stomach until he was lingering over her mound. He pushed her legs apart. Katherine twisted beneath him when he nibbled the bundle of nerves behind the thin material of her panties.

Joseph, holding her still, hooked a finger in her panties and slid them down her thighs. In seconds, she was completely naked, completely vulnerable, and desperately ready.

Katherine's body jerked off the floor when Joseph licked her wet pussy and sucked her clit into his mouth. With his tongue, he teased her clit until she was moaning in ecstasy. He growled hungrily while licking, flicking, and sucking every part of her pussy.

"Oh, my *God!*" Katherine cried. She began to tremble uncontrollably and realized that, for the first time, she was about to have an orgasm with someone else in the room. Her legs stiffened, her toes curled, and like a volcano, the boiling lava churning in her core, erupted.

Joseph gave her pussy one last kiss before climbing her trembling body. He cupped her face and kissed her through heavy breaths while Katherine shuddered through the powerful orgasm. Throughout the kiss, the taste of her pleasure made her want him even more.

Joseph stood and unbuttoned his shirt. When he peeled it off and dropped it to the floor, she saw just how fit he was. His muscular arms and strong torso solidified his sexiness.

Katherine rose on her elbows to get a better view, but when he came out of his pants, then his shorts, she wished she hadn't. His large dick popped out like an angry missile.

The quickening of Katherine's breath drew a smirk.

Joseph must've read her thoughts.

He dropped to the floor and crawled over her. When his lips touched hers, she closed her eyes and inhaled his woodsy, masculine scent. Then he reached down, between their bodies.

Katherine froze.

She opened her eyes and tore her lips from his, severing their connection. When she caught his arm, she saw concern in his eyes.

"Are you okay? Do you want me to stop?" He moved to get up, but Katherine stopped him.

"I'm okay," she assured. "It's just that, I-I've never…"

She trailed off.

"Oh."

"Well, I've done other things. You know, when my…"

Joseph put a finger to her lips as if he couldn't bear to hear the rest. "Shh."

Katherine could see a mixture of understanding and fear in his eyes.

He gave her a reassuring smile and kissed her forehead. "Okay, sweetheart."

Joseph grabbed her hand, placed her arm around his neck, and returned his lips to hers. While making love to her mouth, he used his thighs to push her legs apart. Katherine trembled with anticipation as he slid his hand between them and grabbed himself. Soon, she felt the thick tip of him rubbing her wet opening. With the smooth head of his dick, Joseph massaged her clit and everything around it.

The pleasure caused Katherine to moan, and she found herself thrusting her hips toward him. Even though she was afraid, she needed him more than the very air she was breathing.

Joseph raised his head and looked into her eyes. With a tremble in his voice, he whispered, "Hold on to me."

Katherine wrapped her arms around him and pressed her fingers to the muscles in his back. With their eyes locked, Joseph positioned the head of his dick on her slick pussy. In one thrust, he pushed inside, shattering the proof of her innocence.

Katherine dug her fingers in his back and wailed like a wounded animal. She nearly bit her tongue. The pain was sharp, more than she'd anticipated.

"It gets better, sweetheart. I promise," Joseph assured.

With care, he eased out, then returned slowly. When he repeated the action a few more times, Katherine was grateful to learn he was telling the truth. The pain eased. A few more times, she found herself not only welcoming his invasion, but craving it. Every stroke gifted her with a pain and pleasure combination that made her toes curl.

Katherine wrapped her legs around his waist and thrust upward. He was stretching her, filling her completely, and she wanted more.

Joseph's moans vibrated near her ear. "That's it, sweetheart. Take all of me."

"Yes!" Katherine gasped. Their connection and his closeness were dragging her down the rabbit hole. At that moment, she was eating, sleeping, and drinking all things Joseph. He was the most important thing in her world.

She grabbed his ass, jerked her hips, and yanked the love from his dick.

"Oh, God, Joseph!"

Katherine was well aware that the sounds coming from her were less than ladylike, but she couldn't help it. Joseph was shattering her pride with his big, hard manhood. In one night, he'd transformed her into a wanton, hungry succubus.

Joseph slid his arm behind her neck and held her close as he plunged into her like it was his life's work. Katherine felt a quickening in her belly. Every nerve ending excited. Her entire body convulsed as she braced herself for what was sure to be a massive release. Her heart raced, her breathing stopped, and she exploded. Katherine dug her fingers in Joseph's ass and screamed through a crippling orgasm.

"Oh, fuck, baby!" Joseph cursed.

The swollen walls of Katherine's womanhood convulsed around his dick as he pulsed hot cum into her pussy. Joseph collapsed on the floor beside her and rested his head on her chest. His breathing was labored. Katherine pushed her fingers through his sweat-dampened hair and held him tight as he quivered next to her.

"Are you okay? Joseph asked. "How do you feel?"

Katherine kissed the top of his head and sighed. "I feel like a woman."

CHAPTER 15
JOSEPH

Joseph woke to the sound of soft breathing. Katherine was in a deep sleep with her head resting on his chest. With her in his arms, he felt like a master of the universe. With everything she'd been through, all the pain, betrayal, and degradation, he was honored that she'd given him such a precious gift.

Almost thirty minutes had gone by, and Joseph was still unable to look away. Katherine was stunning; that much was certain. But she was also kind, funny, and incredibly intelligent. At school, he'd admired her from a distance. Yet, he truly hadn't known just how beautiful she was on the inside. To him, she'd been just another rich, pretty brat. But she was so much more, and he wanted all of it.

Katherine stirred and rolled to her back. Her lids blinked open to reveal her beautiful oceanic eyes. She focused on him and smiled. "Good morning."

Joseph lowered his head and kissed her lips. "Good morning, sweetheart."

Katherine tucked her hair behind her ear and sat up. "What time is it?"

"Nine."

"Has Rick called?"

"No, sweetheart, but I'm sure we'll hear from him soon." Katherine moved to stand, but Joseph caught her by the waist. "Where are you going?"

She giggled and tried to wriggle herself free. "I gotta pee."

Joseph held her captive. "You gotta what?" he teased.

"Joseph!" Katherine squealed.

"*Joseph!*" he mocked.

She tried to wrestle her way out of his hold, but Joseph laughed and held her tight.

"I'm going to piss all over your plush carpet," Katherine threatened.

"I usually go to dinner at my mom's on Sundays. Will you join me?"

Katherine squirmed and tried to pry his fingers from her waist. "Joe, I have to pee."

"Dinner?"

Katherine nodded frantically. "Yes!" she blurted with desperation.

Joseph released her and chuckled when she scurried to the bathroom. He watched her, admiring her perfect ass until she disappeared inside. He got up and went into the kitchen to make coffee, but a scream from the bathroom sent him in the other direction. Joseph twisted the knob and pushed the door open. Katherine's face was beet-red. She was sitting on the toilet with a horrified look in her eyes.

"What happened?" Joseph asked, looking around the bathroom for whatever had made her scream.

When Katherine looked up at him, Joseph could sense that she was embarrassed.

"It burns," she admitted with a sheepish grin. "It's really sore."

"Oh." Joseph chuckled with relief. "You just need a good soak in a hot bath."

He left the bathroom to give her some privacy. As he walked down the hall, he smiled at the knowledge that he'd done his job and made her his.

KATHERINE

Joseph used his key to open the door to his mother's house, and she must've heard the door because she yelled, "Hey, you two!" from the kitchen.

"Hey, mom."

Katherine entered the living room and made a beeline for the fireplace. On the mantle were pictures of Joseph's family. There were pictures of a very young, very beautiful Emily with her baby boys in each arm. There were a few of Joseph and Jonathan when they were toddlers, and a few when they were teenagers. When they were younger, it was harder to tell them apart. Now, she could identify Joseph with her eyes closed.

"Welcome," Joseph's mom greeted when she entered the living room. She approached Katherine with open arms.

"How are you, Mrs. Storm," Katherine returned while they hugged.

She took a step back and smiled. "I'm doing well. Katherine, please call me Emily."

Katherine nodded her compliance. "You have a beautiful home."

Emily's home was beautifully decorated. The houseplants occupying a corner of the room offered a sense of serenity. The space was warm and inviting. Surely, Joseph had grown up in a more loving home than she could have even dreamt of.

Katherine pointed to a picture of Joseph and Jonathan wrestling in diapers. "Why are they so cute?"

Emily laughed. "Adorable, right? They were such little monsters."

Katherine's mouth flew open. For some reason, she'd assumed Joseph had come out of the womb as the focused, level-headed man that he was now. "Were they really?"

Emily sighed. "Little hulksters… destroyed everything."

Katherine looked at Joseph and giggled. "Little hulksters, huh?"

Joseph shrugged. "She's exaggerating."

"What's up, baby bro!" Jonathan shouted from the archway.

He walked over and gave Joseph a bear hug.

Joseph hugged his brother, then pushed him off. "That's enough. I didn't know you were still here," he told him.

Jonathan grinned. "Interning with the Chicago division of Lehman Brothers."

"It's that great?" Emily grinned from ear to ear. "Both of my babies are home at the same time."

"That is great," Joseph agreed.

Jonathan walked over and pulled Katherine into a hug. "Hello, miss lady. It's good to see you again."

"It's good to see you too, Jonathan."

Katherine smiled, but she could feel her face warming. She was burning with unintentional envy. She would have given anything to have had a family like Joseph's. And somehow, Joseph sensed it.

He pulled her out of his brother's arms and turned her to face him. "You okay, sweetheart?"

Katherine forced a smile. "Of course. I was just thinking how lucky you guys are to have such a loving family."

Katherine looked away, uncomfortable with the pity in Joseph's eyes, and diverted her attention back to the fireplace. She pointed to a picture of a tall, handsome man with a thick, dark mustache. "Is this your dad?"

The pity in Joseph's eyes turned to what looked like sadness. "Yes," he responded with a sigh.

"Katherine, will you help me with drinks?" Emily interjected.

Katherine was studying Joseph's strange reaction when Emily touched her.

"A little help?" Emily urged.

Katherine had struck a nerve and she didn't know why. "Of course." She acquiesced, following their mom in the kitchen.

"Dinner smells delicious," Katherine sighed.

"Thank you."

Emily pulled two wine glasses from a cabinet and two beers out of the refrigerator. "We're having lasagna. Are you in the mood for red or white?"

"Then, I'll go red," Katherine told her, since red was usually paired with Italian food.

"Perfect. I have a Lambrusco I think you'll like. It's not expensive, but it's delicious."

Joseph must have told his mother about her wealthy background.

"I'm sure it is. I love Lambrusco."

Emily grabbed a bottle from a small wine rack on the counter. She used a corkscrew to open the bottle and placed it on the table.

"We'll let that breath a bit," she said, grabbing the beers. "Have a seat. I'll run these to the boys."

Katherine took a seat at the kitchen table and waited for Emily to return. While waiting, she tried to picture her mother standing at the stove, preparing a meal for her family. For the life of her, she couldn't. Emily seemed happy to cook for her sons. Katherine's mother would have stepped over their nutrient deficient corpses before slaving over a hot stove.

"Okay, now. Let's have a drink," Emily said when she returned to the kitchen. She poured two glasses of wine and sat at the table with Katherine. "So, you and Joseph are seeing each other?"

She got right to it.

"Um…I think… Well, yes, we are."

Emily smiled. "I appreciate how you were there for Joseph when Jack died. You know they'd been friends for most of Joseph's life."

Katherine nodded. "Yes. Joseph told me."

"Katherine, you seem like a very nice young woman."

Katherine thanked her, but she sensed there was more to Emily's observation.

Emily took a large sip of wine and sighed. "You guys come from two different worlds. Do you think your differences may be an issue?"

Katherine was sure to look her in the eye when she said, "No, ma'am. I don't. To be perfectly honest, Joseph and I have more in common than you think."

With a wrinkled brow, Emily asked, "Like what?"

"Well, we're both in law school. We're both hard working people who want to make a difference in the world." Katherine smiled. "We both love his cooking, and we both think you're the grooviest mom ever." Katherine raised a brow. "See? A bunch of things in common."

Emily laughed. "Groovy, huh? Well, I'll take it."

Katherine nodded and took a sip of wine. "Mmm. This is good."

Emily grinned. "Mm-hmm, told ya."

Katherine stayed in the kitchen while Emily finished dinner. While the twins hung out in the living room, she and Joseph's mom finished the entire bottle of wine. Needless to say, dinner was filled with a lot of giggling.

CHAPTER 16
JOSEPH

Joseph propped Katherine up on the wall and unlocked the door to his apartment. Once he got the door open, he lifted her over his shoulder.

Whew!" she whooped as he carried her inside. When he closed the door, she wiggled out of his hold and slid down his body. "I can walk, Mr. Storm."

Joseph chuckled and held her by the shoulders until she was steady on her feet. "Well, I wasn't sure when you fell up the stairs."

"Ha-ha."

Katherine stumbled to the sofa and collapsed. Joseph shook his head and walked over. He couldn't believe how drunk she and his mother had gotten at dinner. Together, they were a riot. After dinner, he'd gathered Katherine and left Joseph to deal with their drunk mother.

"Come on, drunk lady," he said, reaching down to pick her up.

Katherine shook her head, grabbed him by his shirt, and pulled him on the couch. "Not so fast, sexy man. Come here and kiss me."

Faster than any drunk person should have been able, she climbed on his lap and kissed him. With clumsy fingers, she tried to unbutton his shirt, but Joseph caught her hands.

"Whoa!"

She lifted her head and frowned. "Come, Joseph. Stop playing hard to get."

He laughed and stood, lifting her with him. "Let's get you to bed."

"*Joseph!*" she whined as he carried her to the bedroom.

"Yeah, yeah. You've gone from virgin to vixen in less than twenty-four hours," he muttered.

Joseph sat her on the bed. When she fell back on the mattress and groaned, he dropped to one knee and took off her shoes. By the time he stripped her down to her bra and panties, Katherine was fast asleep.

He went into the bathroom and grabbed some aspirin, then to the kitchen to get a glass of water. He went back in the room and put both on the nightstand. "Katherine?"

She opened her eyes, but she wasn't focusing on anything in particular.

Joseph slipped an arm under her and lifted her off the bed. He pulled the sheet and blanket from under and positioned her on the pillow. Katherine closed her eyes and tried to get comfortable, but Joseph couldn't let her doze just yet.

He opened the bottle and poured out two aspirin. "Take this," he urged.

Katherine groaned. "Mm-mm."

Joseph lifted her head and held the aspirin in front of her mouth. "Take this, sweetheart."

"Noooo, I forgot how to swallow," she whined.

"We'll see about that." Joseph pushed the aspirin into her mouth then put the glass of water to her lips.

Katherine made a face, but she swallowed both pills.

He placed the glass on the nightstand and allowed her to lie down. "Good girl," he praised as he covered her with the blanket.

After a kiss to the forehead, Joseph left, turning the light off on the way out. He went into the kitchen and grabbed a beer from the fridge, then grabbed the phone from the receiver and dialed his mother's number.

"How's mom?" he asked when his brother answered.

"Passed out," Jonathan responded with a chuckle. "The ladies really tied one on."

Joseph laughed. "You're telling me. Katherine's out like a light."

Joseph enjoyed his beer while having a short conversation with his brother. When they were done, he tossed the empty bottle in the trash and pushed play on the answering machine. After two miscellaneous messages, there was a message from Rick Bolin—he'd secured search warrants for her parents' home and Robert Chase's office.

Joseph had mixed feelings. It was good news for the victims, but for Katherine, it was going to be an atomic bomb to her private life. Between law enforcement and the newspapers, her entire world was about to be turned upside down.

"Got a couple more for you," Janice said as she dropped the small boxes on his desk.

Joseph looked up from the legal briefs he'd been poring over all morning and smiled. "Gee, thanks."

"Mr. Carlton wants you to sit in on a deposition at 11," she told him, shamelessly leaning over his desk. She had to know that her very low-cut blouse was not securing her massive tits.

Janice was a paralegal and assistant to Andrew Hamlin, the senior partner he was assigned to. She'd been aggressively hitting on him since he started his internship.

"Thanks," Joseph responded. He dipped his head back into the legal briefs and avoided Janice's anything but subtle advances.

Her words came out breathy. "Well, if you need anything at all, you just let me know."

"I'm good, thanks," Joseph assured her without looking up.

Seconds after Janice left, one of the firm's receptionists entered. "Joseph, there's a man with your face waiting for you in the lobby."

Joseph looked up and laughed. "Send him back, please."

"Will do."

She left and a few minutes later, his brother walked in. "What's up, bro?" Joseph greeted.

"I need two thousand dollars," Jonathan blurted unceremoniously.

Joseph dropped his pen and looked up at his brother. "What?"

"I need two grand, bro."

Joseph felt his face twist into a frown. "Why do you need that much money? Are you in trouble?"

Jonathan blew out a frustrated breath. "Of course not. Am I ever in trouble?"

Joseph leaned back in his chair and waited for his brother to explain his reasons for needing such a large sum of money.

Jonathan sighed and took a seat in the chair in front of his desk. "There's this company called Microsoft. Rumor is, they're about merge with IBM. I'm gonna make an invest for both of us."

Joseph chuckled. "No way, man."

Two thousand dollars didn't come easy for him. His job at Ford and his internship barely allowed for dinner and a movie after he paid for school and rent. He wasn't about to invest the little money he'd saved into some unknown company.

Jonathan leaned over his desk and gave him a stern look. "Joe, this is a sure thing."

Joseph shook his head. "It's the stock market," he scoffed.

"Bro, you know me better than anyone. It that not so?"

"That is so," Joseph admitted.

"Have I ever been known to be impulsive or irresponsible?"

Joseph didn't answer because Jonathan already knew is answer. Like Joseph, his twin was responsible and driven. Both were determined to give their mom a better life. If his twin wanted his money, he would certainly invest it in something that he truly believed in.

"That's a lot of money, Jon," Joseph pointed out with a sigh.

"I know. I just need you to trust me."

Jonathan had a passion for business, and he was super sharp. If

Joseph were to trust anyone with his money, it would be the brilliant man with which he'd shared their mother's womb.

Joseph dropped his head in his hands and pushed his fingers through his hair.

"Trust me," Jonathan asserted.

Joseph nodded and grabbed his briefcase from the floor. He opened it and pulled out his checkbook. He wrote the check and handed it over. To say he was reluctant would've been an understatement. He didn't have a lot of money, and no matter how brilliant, his brother was placing a bet on the stock market, and the stock market was anything but a sure thing.

"You're not gonna regret this, Joe."

"Mm-hmm. I'd better not," Joseph grumbled.

Jonathan stuffed the check in his front pocket and stared past Joseph with a frown. "Hey, isn't that your ole lady's dad?"

Joseph swiveled around and looked up at the TV to see what he was talking about. It was breaking news—footage of Katherine's father being taken out of his home in handcuffs. The Feds had raided his house. Some exited carrying boxes of what Joseph assumed were the incriminating files that Katherine had told Rick Bolin about.

"And so it begins," Joseph muttered under his breath.

KATHERINE

Halfway to the copy machine, Katherine noticed that people were staring. She'd chosen an internship at Kaplan and Harlow, a small boutique law firm that specialized in Immigration and Civil Rights. So, it wasn't hard to see that she was being closely watched by the small group of employees.

She'd seen the news coverage of her father being arrested. She understood their curiosity, but they could have been a bit more discreet as opposed to outright gawking. Katherine made her copies and ignored all the eyes burning into her. Once she was done, she hurried to her office, making sure to avoid eye contact with anyone along the way.

She entered her borrowed office, which was more like a storage room, and closed the door. She leaned over her desk, gasping for air as her breath quickened. Her eyes burned with tears as she thought about what was ahead. She would have to testify in court. Deservedly, her family's name was about to be dragged through the mud and since she was also a Chase, she was certain to get stained.

Katherine jumped upright when the door opened. She tried hard to compose herself but failed. As soon as Henrietta, the receptionist, stepped inside, Katherine began to hyperventilate. She was a crying, heaving mess.

"Oh, child." Henrietta closed the door, hurried over to Katherine, and wrapped her arms around her. "What you must've have gone through in that house," she whispered.

Henrietta's assumption was correct, but she truly had no idea of the hell she'd endured.

Katherine held on to Henrietta and sobbed. Henrietta rubbed her back while slowly rocking her from side to side. "Shhh. Don't cry. This mess will blow over before you know it."

Katherine nodded and wiped her face. "I hope so."

She stood straight and worked to pull herself together. Of course, Henrietta was wrong, but she still felt better when it came out of her mouth.

"I'm sorry, Henrietta. Did you need something?"

"Oh, yes. You have a phone call. You can take it on line three."

Katherine placed her hand on Henrietta's shoulder and smiled. "Thank you."

"You're welcome. I'll leave you to it."

Henrietta left and closed the door behind her. Katherine took a deep breath and grabbed the receiver. "This is Katherine Chase."

"Katherine, leave now." Joseph's voice on the other end was soothing.

"Joseph, everyone in my office is—"

"Katherine, leave!" he reiterated. "Don't go out the front. There are reporters there. I'm leaving the office now. In ten minutes, go out the back. I'll be there waiting."

Katherine nodded. "I'll be there."

CHAPTER 18

JOSEPH

Joseph was grateful that the reporters didn't know about him, or where he lived, when he pulled into the parking lot adjacent to his apartment building. He parked and ran around to open Katherine's door.

"Let's get inside and get you a drink."

Katherine got out and placed her hand in his. She pulled him close and looked up at him. "We knew this would get ugly, but it'll be okay."

Joseph kissed the top of her head. The fact that she was trying to reassure him made her more endearing. "Come on, sweetheart. Let's go inside."

He threw his arm over her shoulder and walked her toward the building. Katherine froze when they got to the entrance and found her mother waiting, dressed to the nines with a full face of makeup. But if looks could kill, they'd both be dead.

"Mom?"

"Are you happy with yourself?" her mother hissed as she closed the distance between them.

Katherine stepped forward, just out of Joseph's grasp. "As a matter of fact, I—"

Before she could finish, her mother hauled off and slapped her across the cheek. "You have destroyed this family!"

Katherine recoiled and glared at her mother. "This family?" she challenged. "We were never a family! At least, I wasn't. I was nothing more than prey to that predatory piece of shit you call a husband." Katherine turned to Joseph and stuck her hand out. "Let's go."

Joseph took her hand. Without so much as a single glance, they walked past her mother, leaving her standing on the stoop. Although, if he had to confess, he was secretly hoping that Katherine retaliated with a slap of her own.

When they entered the apartment, Katherine walked into the living room and looked out of the window.

"She gone?" Joseph asked.

"I think so."

He grabbed a beer from the fridge. "I wonder how she found you."

Katherine left the window and walked into the kitchen. "My mother has a bevy of resources at her disposal. Finding would be a piece of cake."

Joseph grabbed a bottle of red wine, poured Katherine a glass, and handed it to her. "Today must've been hard. Are you okay?"

"I am," she assured, taking a sip.

Joseph watched her for a bit to see if she was just acting like everything was okay. When he couldn't tell one way or the other, he opened the freezer and pulled out a package of ground beef. "How about spaghetti tonight?"

Katherine smiled. "Spaghetti sounds amazing. I'm going to watch you cook it so I can make it for you someday."

Joseph chuckled. "Oh, yeah? You gonna cook for me?"

Katherine walked around the table, snaked her arms around his neck, and rose to her toes for a kiss. "Yep," she confirmed, raising on her toes for a kiss.

Joseph wrapped his arms around her waist and lowered his lips to hers. He captured her tongue and deepened the kiss. The feel of her lips had his cock throbbing and aching to be inside her. Joseph caressed her body, ready to take her to bed when the shrill ringing of the phone caused Katherine to jump and sever their connection.

"I'll get it," Joseph offered.

Whoever it was, he was going to get rid of them so he could enjoy the pleasure of ridding Katherine of her clothes and licking every part of her.

He walked over to the counter and grabbed the receiver. "Hello?"

"Hi. This is Yolanda Greer. I'm looking for Katherine Chase."

"One moment, please." Joseph aimed the phone at Katherine. "It's somebody named Yolanda Greer."

Katherine grabbed the phone. She seemed surprised by the call. "This is Katherine."

After a few seconds, she apologized to the person on the other end. As she listened quietly to the caller, Joseph watched her expression go from curious to dejected.

"I understand, Yolanda. Thank you for calling."

Katherine hung up the phone and dropped her head with a sigh. It was obvious that Yolanda Greer hadn't delivered good news.

Joseph rubbed her shoulders and turned her to face him. "What is it?"

"My internship has been terminated," she revealed.

"Oh, no, Katherine. I'm so sorry." Joseph wrapped her in his arms. Thought it was unlikely, he was hoping to provide some comfort.

Katherine rested her head on his chest and swiped a tear from her cheek. "She said the reporters were disruptive, but she did say there would be a place for me once all of this is over."

"That's good. It'll be fine." Joseph guided her to the table and pulled out a chair. "Sit. Have some more wine."

Katherine pushed the glass to the side and put her head down on the table. Joseph grabbed his beer and sat across from her. He had to figure something out. Her sadness was crippling.

"I have an idea," he announced.

Katherine raised her head and pushed her hair out of her face. "What's that?" she asked.

Joseph could hear the stress and frustration in her tone. "I was thinking we should get away for the weekend. We could drive to Wisconsin, do some hiking and fishing. We could leave tomorrow."

Katherine's brows wrinkled. "Leave tomorrow? Tomorrow's Tuesday. How are you going to leave? You have to go into the office."

Joseph waved off her concerns. "They can do without me for a few days. They recruited me. I'll be fine." He said it, but he wasn't sure it was true. He hoped they wouldn't take his spot away for going missing for a few days. "Like I said, we could sleep under the stars at night and fish during the day."

"Fishing?" Her face twisted into a frown as if she could actually smell the fish. "Joseph, I'm not sleeping under no stars and not touching any smelly fish."

Now, it was Joseph's face that twisted into a frown.

Katherine raised a brow. "I have a better idea," she said with a mischievous grin.

Joseph placed his elbows on the table and linked his fingers. "Let's hear it."

"I say, we do an extended weekend in the Bahamas."

"What?" Joseph gasped. "We can't afford that."

Katherine smiled. "I can. My credit cards still work."

Joseph shook his head. "The Feds are gonna be freezing your dad's accounts."

"They haven't yet. I say we prepay for everything with my credit card. So, if they cut it off, everything is already paid for."

Joseph sipped his beer. "That's crazy," he scoffed.

"Why is it so crazy? You were right. I need to get away. Soon, I'll have to testify. Eventually, the press is gonna find me. My life is gonna be turned upside down. Why not seize the moment?" Katherine stood and walked around the table. She sat on his lap and cupped his face. "Please, honey."

Joseph was caught in her hypnotic blue gaze. How could he resist? "Okay. Let's do it."

Katherine's eyes lit up with excitement. "Really?"

Joseph gave her a peck on the lips. "Really," he confirmed. "Let's go to the Bahamas."

Katherine squealed with glee and hugged his neck. She pulled back with a giant smile on her face. "You know what?"

"What's that, sweetheart?"

"We're going in style. I'm gonna show you how the rich and superficial live."

"Okay," Joseph muttered. "Show me how the other half live."

Katherine bounced up and down on his lap, reminding him of the plan he'd had before the phone rang. Intent on feeling her warm, tight insides, Joseph stood, lifting her with him, and carried her off to the bedroom.

CHAPTER 19
JOSEPH

“I could have driven us to the airport.” Joseph had never ridden in a limo before. He built cars for a living, and he’d seen better.

“I know, honey. But why would you?”

Joseph shrugged and looked out of the window. “I guess you’re right.”

Katherine moved across the limo to take the seat next to him. She covered his hand with her own. “Joseph, don’t worry so much. Everything is prepaid. They can’t pull the rug from under us.”

“Are you sure?”

“I’m sure,” she promised.

Joseph frowned and leaned closer to the window. They had just passed the exit for the airport.

“Hey, driver!” he called.

Katherine leaned forward to see what he what he saw. “What is it, Joseph?”

“We passed O’Hare.”

“Oh, no.” Katherine smiled. “We’re going to a different hanger.”

“A different hanger? What do you mean a different hanger?”

"You'll see. Honey, try to relax."

Joseph sighed. "Okay, fine. I'm relaxed."

For Katherine, he would try.

He took a deep breath and sank into the plush leather. Soon, they were turning. They drove through a few gates and came to a halt in what looked like a big parking lot. Joseph leaned forward and looked out of opposite window.

"Holy shit!" Joseph cursed.

There was an airplane with "CHASE" painted on the body.

The back door opened, and the driver reached in to assist Katherine. She got out, and Joseph got out after her. He looked up at the airplane. He never dreamt he'd be traveling on a private plane.

Joseph walked to the rear of the car and waited for the driver to pop the trunk. Katherine joined him, grabbed his hand, and pulled him away from the car. "The bags are being handled. Come on."

She led him up the steps to the aircraft and stepped in. Joseph stepped in after her, and he felt like he'd entered another dimension. He'd entered a world of supple leather covered in mink throws, a beautiful flight attendant carrying a tray of champagne, and more space than he'd ever seen on an airplane. There even was even a full bar at the rear of the aircraft.

"Miss Chase, Mr. Storm, welcome aboard," the flight attendant greeted with a smile.

"Thank you, Bernice. It's good to see you again," Katherine replied, grabbing two glasses of champagne.

Joseph smiled, gave her a nod, and followed Katherine down the aisle. She took a seat in a huge leather lounger and patted the one next to her. When he sat, she handed him the glass of champagne.

"This is something else," Joseph admitted.

"Yeah. It is pretty nice."

Joseph looked over at Katherine. She was an anomaly. She'd been surrounded by luxury most of her life. She'd gone from a mansion and vacation homes to his shitty apartment. And she never once made him feel like it wasn't good enough.

Bernice approached with a plate of warm towels. "Can I get you something to snack on before takeoff?"

Katherine shook her head. "I'm fine."

Bernice turned to Joseph with the question in her eyes.

"I could use a snack," Joseph responded. He might as well live it up.

"Right away, Mr. Storm."

"Thank you. Oh, and may I have a beer?"

"Certainly, Mr. Storm."

When Bernice walked away, the captain entered the cabin. "Miss Chase, Mr. Storm, welcome aboard. We'll be taking off in a few minutes. It's pretty clear out there. I've estimated a flight time of three hours and twenty minutes."

"Thanks, Bruce."

The pilot nodded and disappeared into the cockpit. Joseph handed Katherine his glass of champagne. "That's all you, sweetheart."

Katherine chuckled. "I'll take it."

She sat both glasses on a table in front of them and caressed his face. "Thank you for this," she whispered before giving him the sweetest kiss.

Joseph laughed. "I don't know why you're thanking me. You did all this."

When Katherine pulled back, her expression was serious. "Joseph, I'm thanking you for being here with me."

Joseph pushed his fingers through her silky strands and pulled her face closer to his. "I'm here because I love you, Katherine."

Katherine gasped. "You love me?"

Joseph ran his thumb along her jaw. "I love you," he confirmed.

Her beautiful eyes clouded with moisture. "I love you too."

Joseph cupped her face in his hands. "You love me too?"

Katherine nodded. "I do."

Joseph kissed her, gently sucking her bottom lip. With his

tongue, he broke through and connected with hers. He kissed her, knowing that he would never be as lucky as he was at that very moment.

KATHERINE

JOSEPH STEPPED INTO THE MASTER BEDROOM IN HER FAMILY'S BEACH house. "This is incredible."

"It is," Katherine had to admit.

The house had perfect view of a clear blue ocean lined with powdery white sand. Their beach house was private property that included amenities from a nearby luxury resort. Katherine slid back the sheers and opened the patio doors. She closed her eyes and welcomed the warm breeze that invaded the room.

Joseph walked up and hugged her from behind. "This is truly a paradise."

"Miss Chase?"

Katherine turned toward the familiar voice. "Fiona, hello. How are you?"

"I'm still here, blessed and highly favored." Fiona's warm Caribbean drawl always made Katherine smile. "And who is this handsome man?"

"Fiona, this is Joseph Storm. Joseph, this is Miss Fiona. She takes care of the house."

Fiona smiled. "Your man?"

Katherine chuckled nervously. She'd never referred to him as her man.

"Well, child?" Fiona prodded.

"Yeah, well?" Joseph chimed.

"I—well, yes. This is my man," Katherine declared.

Joseph grabbed her and kissed the top of her head. "Well, there it is."

"Now that that's settled, I have prepared lunch for you on the patio."

"Thanks, Fiona. Well, be down in a bit."

"No rush," she responded with a wink. "It'll keep."

Joseph walked through the dancing sheers and stood on the terrace. "I'm gonna like being your man," he joked.

Katherine laughed. "Enjoy while you can. All this is temporary."

Joseph reentered the room and walked over to her. He cupped her face and kissed her lips. "No, it's not, sweetheart. I'm gonna give you all this and more."

"You are?" she asked with beaming admiration.

Joseph grinned with a raised brow. "I'll have to. You're not gonna make any money in immigration," he teased.

Katherine slapped his arm and laughed. "You're probably right. We need to get you back to work."

Joseph chuckled and walked over to his suitcase. "I'm gonna grab a shower and put on some trunks." While going through his things, he frowned and looked up. "How is it you only brought one tiny bag? "I've never heard of a woman under-packing."

Katherine laughed. "I have a wardrobe that stays here."

"Well, damn, Miss Chase. Must be nice."

Katherine shrugged. "There's so much more to life than material things. I know that better than anyone."

"So true."

He pulled his swim trunks from his suitcase and tossed them on the bed. He lifted his shirt over his head, capturing her full attention. Joseph had the kind of body a woman wanted to be under all the time. His muscular torso was a treat for the eyes and the thin hair on his chest was soft and masculine. Katherine found herself shamelessly gawking by the time he'd stepped out of his pants.

Joseph looked up and found her staring and grinned. "Can I help you with something?"

"So much," Katherine whispered.

Joseph laughed and disappeared into the bathroom. Katherine was about to go to the other bedroom to find her swimsuit when she heard the shower. Then it occurred to her that she needed a shower too, and the thought of spreading lather all over Joseph's Adonis-like form was too much to resist.

CHAPTER 20
JOSEPH

Joseph wanted to appreciate the beauty of the Caribbean Sea, but he couldn't seem to look away from Katherine in her tiny yellow bikini. She was relaxing in a lounge chair with her eyes covered by shades. Her long, black hair was tied in a tight bun at the top of her head. Joseph had never seen her more relaxed.

Joseph knew all too well what was waiting for her back in Chicago. Katherine would have to testify against her own father. And, horrible or not, he was still her father. She was about to single-handedly sully their family's undeserved "good name." There was no way testifying would be easy, but Katherine was strong, just, and brave. She would do what she needed to do the protect any child that could fall prey to Robert Chase and men like him.

Joseph was proud of her. Not only was he going to make sure she had the time of her life on their weekend away, he was also going to be by her side to protect her from any and everything that threatened her happiness.

Joseph reached over and touched her arm. "Sweetheart, are you awake?"

"Nope. I'm up." Her tone was relaxed and lazy.

"Let's go for a swim."

Katherine groaned. "Nah, I'm good. You go."

Joseph had a picture of them in the ocean and her wet, slippery body sliding up and down his, and he was about to make it happen. He grabbed his beer and stood over her sun-kissed body. Before he could talk himself out of it, he tilted the bottle and poured beer all over her half-naked body.

Katherine screamed and jumped to her feet. *"Joseph!"*

Joseph laughed and jumped back when she took a swing at him. "I guess you got go rinse off!"

When he took off toward the water, Katherine took off after him. She chased him into the water and jumped on his back. She tried to put him in a headlock, but he was too slippery, so she couldn't get a grip and fell in the water.

Joseph scooped her out of the water. "Are you okay?" he asked through hysterical laughter.

Katherine wiped her face. She shook the water off like a puppy and bared her fangs. "I'm gonna kill you, Joseph!"

"No, sweetheart. You gonna give me some luv'n."

Joseph grabbed her leg and wrapped it around his waist. He gripped the back of her head and pulled her face to his until their lips touched. They kissed with intent. Joseph slid his hand down her back until he reached the string of her bikini. He reached one goal by freeing her tits from the tiny triangle bikini top. Then, he set out to reach another and untied one side of the bottom.

Without breaking the kiss, Katherine reached down and worked his cock out of his swim trunks. She climbed his body and positioned herself for his entry. Joseph gripped her ass and held her with one hand while using the other to guide his cock into her warm pussy.

Katherine exhaled a sharp breath and grabbed his back, pressing her fingers into his flesh. Joseph held her ass and allowed the wave to guide his every stroke. Inside her, he found salvation. With each thrust, her tight canal stripped away at a lifetime of remorse. He needed her. And when they came to an explosive ending together, Joseph realized that he wouldn't make it without her.

CHAPTER 21
KATHERINE

KATHERINE leaned against the rail and stared out into the sunset. Rays of orange and yellow bounced off the blue water of the sea, creating a vibrant shade of purple. If she'd ever seen anything so beautiful, she didn't remember it.

She had dinner prepared on her father's yacht. It had been the most romantic evening of her life. In fact, the entire weekend felt like a dream. She and Joseph ate, slept, and breathed each other under the warmth of the Caribbean sun. But it would all be over soon. It was their last night in the Bahamas. The next day, a luxurious aircraft would be returning them to the hell they'd fled.

Joseph moved behind her and wrapped and arm around her waist. "What's on your mind, sweetheart?"

Katherine didn't want to spoil their evening with real world problems. "I was thinking we should take the tender over to the resort. Fiona says they're having a beach party tonight."

Joseph pulled her hair out of the way and kissed her neck. "Sounds like fun. But what were you really thinking about?"

"Home." Katherine sighed. "I was thinking about what's waiting for me back home."

Joseph turned her around to face him and caressed her cheek. "I know you're worried, sweetheart, but you don't have to be. You survived a nightmare, and it didn't break you. Katherine, you're the strongest person I know."

The love in his eyes made her believe his words.

"Yeah?" she asked.

"Yes, love, and we're gonna get through this together. I'm with you all the way."

Katherine smiled and caressed his jaw. "We're in this together, huh?"

"Yes," Joseph implored.

Katherine took a sidestep out of his grasp. If he wanted them to be one, it couldn't be one-sided. "Why do you shut me down every time I mention your dad?"

Joseph knew about her tragic life. He knew what she'd endured as a child growing up in her father's house. He was privy to the good, the bad, and the ugly. But he'd yet to be forthcoming with the intimacies of his life.

"Whenever I mention your dad, you shut me down, and it's not just you. Your mom and your brother are just as dismissive. Tell me why?"

Joseph dropped his head and gripped the rails until his knuckles turned white. Katherine reached up and placed her hand on his back and kneaded his tense muscles in hopes of bringing him comfort. She didn't know anything about his father, mainly because he refused to share his feelings.

"Tell me why, Joseph?" Katherine prodded.

Joseph took a deep breath and turned his back to her. Something was weighing heavily on him, but he struggled to talk about it. But Katherine was going to know, and she would know before they went any further. If they were in it together, they had to be together completely. They couldn't do that with secrets.

"Joseph?"

His breathing increased. He held on to the rail as if he were in distress.

"My father was not a good person," Joseph whispered. He released the rail, turned around, and gestured toward the deck furniture. "Come. Sit down."

Katherine took a seat, and he sat next to her.

"My father was very abusive to all of us, but especially my mom. For most of her adult life, my mother was miserable, only finding joy in her children. When we got older, Jon and I were able to keep my dad from hurting my mother. When we started college, she built up the courage to leave him. And she did."

Joseph's eyes welled with unshed tears. Katherine rubbed his back in hopes of soothing his pain.

"But he found her. He stalked her and threatened her until she felt like she was losing her mind. He promised to kill her if she didn't return to him, and he tried to make good on that promise. One night, I came home from school to surprise my mom. I barely made it up the front porch before I heard the screams. I kicked her door open. He was yelling so loud, he didn't even hear me come in."

Joseph dropped his head and sobbed in his hands.

"It's okay, honey," Katherine whispered with tears pooling in her own eyes.

"N-no," Joseph choked. "It's not."

Katherine wrapped an arm around him and kissed the top of his head.

"He was beating my mother with a bat. She was a bloody mess. He beat her so bad, I couldn't recognize her. I pushed him away from her, but when I went to check on her, he hit me with the bat. I fell on my mom, and he hit me again. I was dazed, but I managed to get up. My mom was crying, begging me to run, but I wasn't leaving that house without her. When my dad swung the bat at me again and missed, I tackled him into a glass table and punched. I stunned him, but he was still fighting. He grabbed a shard of glass, stabbed me in the side, and pushed me off him. He climbed over me, prepared to stab me again, but I kick him and scrambled to my feet. Somehow, I managed to take him down. I started hitting him. At first, I just wanted to subdue him, but I looked over at my mother's lifeless form and an unstoppable rage took over."

Joseph raised his head, his eyes red from crying. It was a side of him she'd never seen. He was so hurt, so broken, Katherine would have done anything, given up anything to make the pain go away. She'd once thought Joseph's family was perfect, but she was realizing that no family was.

He swiped a tear from his cheek, inhaled a deep breath, and looked her directly in the eye. "When it was all over, Katherine, I had killed my father."

He paused for a breath, but it didn't seem to help. Joseph was inconsolable. Katherine pulled his head to her chest and held him tight.

"I beat... I beat my father to death!" he cried.

Katherine rocked him gently while rubbing his head. "You had to, honey. You had no other choice. He would've killed you and your mother." Tears trickled from her eyes as she kissed his head. "You saved your mother's life."

"I know, but the guilt... it eats at me. Every time I look into my brother's eyes, I think about how I deprived him of a father."

"Was your brother angry at you?"

"On the contrary, Jonathan said if he'd been in my shoes, he would have killed him too."

"And I believe him." Katherine raised Joseph's head, forcing him to look at her. "I know it hurts, honey. But try imagine how much pain you'd be in if it was your mother who died that night." She wiped his face dry and smiled. "Listen here, Joe. This is our last night on the beautiful island, and we're not gonna waste it shedding tears for the man that tried to kill you and that amazing woman you call Mom."

Joseph blessed her with a boyish grin that surprisingly made him look even more sexy. "You got it, sweetheart." He pulled her onto his lap captured her lips for a quick kiss. "Come on. Let's hop in the tender and go to that party."

CHAPTER 22
KATHERINE

Katherine noticed an envelope on the floor when she entered the apartment. She stepped over it and carried her groceries bags to the kitchen counter. She thought of checking the answering machine but changed her mind. Lately, all the recordings were vicious threats from anonymous men.

After putting the groceries away, Katherine walked over and picked up the envelope. She opened it and pulled out a note with letters made out with cuttings from newspaper:

"You'll never make it to court, bitch!"

Katherine folded the note and tossed it in the kitchen drawer with the rest of the written threats she'd received. She and Joseph had returned from the Bahamas six weeks ago. That was when the calls and letters started.

When it was all said and done, the FBI had arrested twenty-seven men in connection with her father's pedophilia racket. Charges ranged from kidnapping and trafficking to rape and assault. Some, including her aunt, were charged with conspiracy. Needless to say, there were a lot of pissed off child molesters who didn't want Katherine to testify to what she saw, but she wasn't deterred. Every last one of those monsters deserved to be tried and convicted. She'd been in and out of the U.S. Attorney's office for weeks. She had given written statements, recorded statements, and committed to testifying.

Katherine grabbed a bottle of wine from the rack and a glass from the cabinet. She was set to pour herself a tall glass of wine when the phone rang. She wanted to ignore it, but it could have been Joseph calling.

Katherine exhaled, left the glass on the counter, and grabbed the receiver. "Hello?"

"Katherine Chase?"

"Yes, this is Katherine."

"Hold, please," the female voice said on the other end.

Seconds later Katherine heard crying.

"Katie?"

It was Gabby.

"Gabby? What's happened? Are you okay?"

"I've been arrested!" she cried.

Katherine gasped. She could hear the terror in her voice.

"Arrested? For what?"

"I don't know, Katie. They say I'm gonna get deported." Gabby cried hysterically. "I can't go back, Katie. I'll kill myself first."

"Gabby, calm down. I'm gonna get you some help. Keep your mouth closed. Don't say anything to anyone."

Gabby was sobbing on the other end, but Katherine needed her to stay calm. They both knew she was being punished for helping her, even if they had no proof that she had.

"Gabby, not a word to anyone. Do you hear me?"

"Sí, I hear you," she said with a sniffle.

Katherine grabbed a pen and pad from a drawer. "Now, where are you?"

After writing down the details, Katherine hung up. She grabbed her keys and purse and left the apartment. She locked up, ran down the stairs, and left the building. She jogged to the parking lot just in time to see her car being hooked to a tow truck.

Katherine picked up the pace and sprinted to her car. "What are you doing?" she shouted at the tow truck driver. "That's my car!"

The driver looked down at his clipboard. "No, ma'am. According to this, this car belongs to Robert and Elizabeth Chase. And I'm sorry to say, they've repossessed it."

"Son of a bitch!" Katherine screamed. She pushed her fingers through her hair and blew out a frustrated breath. Her parents were assholes, but there was nothing she could do about it. So, she turned around and stomped back to the apartment building.

After dropping her purse on a table beside the front door, she hurried over to the phone, dialed the number for Kaplan and Harlow, and waited. She sighed with relief when Henrietta answered.

"I need your help," Katherine blurted into the phone. "It's important."

JOSEPH

Joseph tucked a few folded boxes under his arm and grabbed a roll of tape. Since Jack's mom couldn't bring herself to do it, he'd offered to pack up his apartment. Katherine was still on the phone; she'd been on the phone since he got home. From what he'd overheard, the Chases' housekeeper was facing deportation.

Joseph gestured toward Jack's apartment to let her know he was leaving.

Katherine told the caller to hold on and covered the mouthpiece. "I'll be over in a few minutes to give you a hand."

Joseph nodded and left the apartment. He used the key Jack left for emergencies to unlock the door. Jack's apartment was immaculate, clearly decorated by a man who understood art. Joseph put the boxes on the floor and looked around. He hadn't the first clue where to begin, but he wanted a beer, so the kitchen was as good a place as any. He grabbed the tape and one of the boxes and went into the kitchen. Looking at Jack's state of the art kitchen, it was hard to tell that they'd lived in the same building. But Jack had been a chef. In the kitchen, he would have nothing but the best.

After he assembled the box, Joseph realized that he needed newspaper to wrap the dishes. He searched the utility closet since that was where he stored his old newspapers. Luckily, he and his friend had that in common. Joseph grabbed the paper and put it on the counter. He pulled the dishes out of the cupboard and wrapped them individually. Because Jack had just enough for a single man, it didn't take long to pack the dishes.

Joseph moved on to the pots and pans which Jack kept in the lower row of cabinets.

He sat on the floor with tears in his eyes and pulled them out, one by one. He was smacked with the memory of his nine-year-old friend digging holes in his mother's backyard to make mud pies. It was then that Jack had revealed that he was going to be the most famous chef in the world. And before he died, he'd been well on his way. Jack had studied all over the world with some of the greatest chefs on the planet. As one of the chefs who'd cooked for Jimmy Carter's Inaugural Ball, he was able to add cooking for a president to his resume.

Jack was talented, ambitious, and dedicated to perfecting his craft. The world suffered a loss when American Airlines Flight 191 crashed to the ground.

KATHERINE

Katherine grabbed sixpack from the fridge. She had a feeling Joseph could use a beer or two. He'd offered to pack Jack's things for Jack's family, but it couldn't have been easy for him. So, she was headed across the hall to give him a hand.

Katherine turned off the living room light and opened the door to leave, but what met her on the other side of the door caused her to scream. A large man in a ski mask lunged at her, grabbing her by the throat. She swung the sixpack at his head, but it didn't deter him. His thick finger squeezed her throat, cutting off her air supply. Katherine was choked into silence, but she kept fighting, yet kicking and punching him was doing no good. She clawed at his fingers and begged with her eyes, but her attacker was relentless. He lifted her off her feet and slammed her body to the floor. A shard from a broken beer bottle pierced her side. Spots of red clouded her vision. She was weak and her arms went limp, but Katherine wasn't ready to die. She felt around the floor until she found a piece of glass and plunged it into her assailant's face. He howled in pain, but he didn't loosen his grip.

"Die, bitch!" he growled.

Katherine felt that death was near. She was in a cloud, no longer able to move her limbs. There was nothing left to do but lie there and die. She closed her eyes and reconciled with the inevitability of her death when she was suddenly granted a reprieve. Her attacker was no longer on top of her. Katherine didn't know how or why; she took the opportunity to gulp as much air as she could.

Assuming she wasn't out of danger, Katherine rolled to her side and searched for her attacker. What she found was Joseph on top of the masked man, inflicting a vicious beating. With every punch given, he shouted, *"Who sent you?"*

Joseph savagely beat the man until urine trickled to the floor. *"Who sent you?"*

"Nobody!" the man cried.

"Bullshit!" Joseph barked. "Not one of those rich bastards would have the balls to do their own dirty work!" Joseph landed a blow to his ribs. "You're gonna tell me who sent you or you're not leaving here alive."

He punched him in the face again.

Katherine jumped at the sound of bones cracking in the man's nose and gasped. "Joseph!"

Joseph whipped his head around and looked at her. What she saw in his eyes was scary. She saw a man capable of keeping his promise if the man didn't give him the name he was asking for.

"He was trying to kill you, Katherine," he snarled. Joseph turned back to the man and struck him again. *"Give me a name!"*

The man must've seen the same thing in Joseph's eyes that Katherine saw because he surrendered and revealed the name of the person who'd dispatched him to their home. Joseph was winded when climbed off the would-be assassin and sat against the wall. He looked up at her and wiped the seat from his forehead.

"Call the police," he instructed through a heavy breath.

Katherine paced outside the courtroom while waiting on Henrietta to arrive. She walked over to the window and looked down at the busy, downtown street for a distraction.

"Katherine."

She turned to the sound of Henrietta's voice and smiled. "Thank you so much for coming. Did you bring the case law?"

Henrietta nodded. "I brought that and more."

Henrietta gestured toward the elevator, just as Colette Kaplan and Jared Harlow stepped off. Katherine's jaw dropped. The senior partners' presence was shocking.

"You're here," she said, stating the obvious.

Colette smiled. "We're here."

Katherine pointed to the courtroom. "That's wonderful. Thank you, but Gabby doesn't have any money." She dropped her head. "I don't have any money."

Colette approached and placed her hand on her shoulder. "No worries, dear. This is what we do. Your friend," she looked down at the file, "Gabriela Rodriguez has a good case. According to Henrietta, she's a material witness in a federal case with several defendants. We believe we can not only stave deportation, but we also have a good chance of getting her released tonight."

"Oh, my God, really?" Katherine gasped. She couldn't hide her excitement as she smiled and grabbed Colette's hand. "Thank you so much." She also thanked Henrietta and Jared.

"You're welcome," Jared responded. "Now, let's go to work."

JOSEPH

"I made it."

"Good. Don't forget, you're in the fourth office on the left. I don't have a name plate, but there's a big picture of a whale on the wall behind the desk."

"I got it, bro. I've mastered the art of being you my entire life. You just be careful."

"Will do." Before hanging up, Joseph exhaled. "Thanks, Jon."

"No need, brother. Do what you gotta do."

Joseph hung up the phone and left his apartment. A twenty-minute drive got him to the upscale Barrington neighborhood. When he arrived at his destination, he parked, snacked on a bag of potato chips, and waited. It was nearly noon by the time anyone besides the household staff came and went.

When a fancy Jaguar pulled out of the driveway and took off down the street, Joseph took off behind him. He followed his target to the tailor, the jewelry store, and even to his coke dealer before he found the perfect place to confront him—a bar where a well-known westside bookie did business. Folks in that area saw a lot but reported very little. No one was willing to bring attention to Money Jack's gambling establishment.

Joseph pulled into the parking lot and parked next to the Jaguar. He slipped on a pair of leather gloves and jumped out at the same time as Larry Crane. When he ran around the car, Larry took one look at him and tried to take off running. Only, he was between two cars with a brick building behind him. Larry would have had to run through him to get away. Joseph could see the contemplation in his eyes, so he punched him before Larry could make an attempt.

Larry bounced off the brick wall and fell to the concrete.

Joseph climbed over him and drilled him with punches. "You sent a man to my house to kill my woman?" he raged through gritted teeth.

Larry tried to fight back, but the preppy, overprivileged man's hands had never seen a day of work. And, at that time, they weren't working in his defense. He was no match. Joseph beat the hell out of him while safely hidden between the two cars. When his arms got tired, he kicked him.

"Stay the fuck away from Katherine!" he said with a kick to Larry's ribs. "This is your only warning!"

Joseph had every intention on walking away, but Larry spit blood from his mouth and laughed. "That bitch will never testify! I won't stand by a watch my dad ruined because she couldn't mind her goddamned business!"

Larry's father, Larry Crane Sr., had been implicated in the fed's pedophilia case.

Larry curled into a ball when Joseph kicked him again.

"Your piece of shit father is a child predator! He deserves to die in jail!"

"Fuck you!" Larry spat. "My father can buy and sell you and that bitch! She'll never make it to a courtroom!"

Joseph dropped to his knees and snaked and arm around Larry's neck. He lifted him in a chokehold and leaned against the building for support. Essentially, Larry was telling him that he wasn't going to stop coming after Katherine until she was dead. Joseph might have believed it to be an idle threat had Larry not already sent an attacker to their home.

He tightened his grip on Larry's neck and wrapped his legs around him to subdue his struggle. Joseph closed his eyes and maintained the hold. He knew what he was about to do. He'd done it before. And, just like then, he felt he had no other choice.

After a few minutes, Larry was no longer struggling. He had gone completely still. He wasn't asleep. He wasn't breathing. Joseph had killed him. He had killed yet another man to protect a woman he loved. Maybe he was a bad man, but just like his father's death, he would have to live with Larry Crane's.

KATHERINE

Katherine smiled when she heard the lock turn. She'd been a bit paranoid since the attempt on her life, but it was safe to assume the next assailant didn't have a key. Joseph walked in and placed his briefcase on the table near the door.

Katherine walked over and slid her arms around his neck. She stood on her toes and gave him a kiss.

Joseph smiled. "Hey, sweetheart. How'd it go in court?"

"Good. The partners actually showed up to represent Gabby. They were able to get her out as a material witness. And after they told the prosecutor about what happened to me, they put her in protective custody."

Joseph raised a brow. "I'm surprised they didn't offer you protective custody."

"They did," Katherine admitted with a grin. "But who's gonna protect me better than you?"

Joseph chuckled and nodded his head toward the kitchen. "What's happening in there?"

Katherine kissed his chin and jogged back into the kitchen. "I'm cooking," she proudly announced.

"*What?*"

Katherine whipped around and glared at him through narrowed eyes. He seemed astonished and a bit scared.

"I made pot roast. Your mother walked me through it."

Joseph chuckled. "Okay, sweetheart. Do I have time to grab a quick shower?"

"Yep. Dinner will be done in ten minutes."

Joseph walked to the back of the apartment. A few minutes later, she heard the shower. Her pot roast only needed a few more minutes. Since Joseph liked eating in front of the TV, she used that time to set dinner trays in front of the sofa. As she was placing napkins and utensils on the trays, a news story caught her attention.

Katherine sat and stared at the television with disbelief. It was reported that Larry Crane had been found dead in the parking lot of a westside bar. Apparently, he was beaten and strangled to death.

Katherine gasped. Her hand flew over her mouth. It hadn't gone over her head that Larry had been murdered within days of her attacker's revelation that Larry was who'd hired him to kill her. Katherine got up and rushed to the bathroom. The shower was still going when she entered without knocking, but Joseph wasn't in the shower. He was sitting on the edge of the tub his head in his hands.

Katherine took one look at him and knew immediately that Joseph was responsible for Larry's death, even if his knuckles hadn't been so badly bruised. When he realized she'd entered the bathroom, he looked up with tears in his eyes. He swiped a tear and cleared his throat.

"Katherine, I..." His voice cracked. "I wasn't planning on killing him, but he..."

His pain was her agony.

Katherine stepped in front of him and cupped his face. "I know, honey." She dropped to her knees and pulled him into her arms. "It's gonna be okay," she whispered. "I promise."

CHAPTER 24
KATHERINE

Joseph held the door open for Katherine to enter the courtroom. She was nervous, but happy to finally get her day in court. The crowded court quieted as they made their way down the aisle. They found a couple of empty seats in the fourth row, but before they could slide into the row, they were waved down by Jake Quinn, the Assistant U.S. State's Attorney.

Katherine and Joseph pivoted and followed Jake to a little room at the back of the courtroom. Katherine assumed he wanted to prep her a little more in anticipation of her testimony, but when they entered the room, he had a looked that worried Katherine.

"What is it?" she asked.

Jake took a deep breath and gestured toward a chair. "Why don't you take a seat?"

Katherine looked at the chair and frowned. "I don't want to sit. What's going on?"

After a sigh, the attorney said, "We're not going to need your testimony anymore."

Katherine was blown away. "What?"

"Your father cut a deal. He's going to not only testify against every defendant, but he's also going to give up offenders we didn't know about."

"What does that mean for him?" Joseph asked.

"Three years in prison and five years of supervised probation."

Katherine clutched her chest. "*What?*"

"I know it's not what you want to hear, but—"

"Of course, it's not what I want to hear! My father abused me and others for years. Now, you're telling me he's gonna get off with a slap on the wrist!"

"He's not getting off, Katherine. In addition to serving his time, your father is about to help convict dozens of pedophiles. Please, try to think of all the children we'll be protecting by taking these monsters off the street."

Katherine rolled her eyes and blew out a frustrated breath. She did, however, notice that Joseph was unusually quiet. She looked over at him and threw her hands up.

"Sweetheart, I understand that you're upset," Joseph said. "In a perfect world, all the bad men would go to prison forever. But this world is not perfect. Sometimes, we gotta take what we can get. Your father is going to prison. He will never navigate in this world the way he's accustomed to. His life is ruined."

Of course, Jake and Joseph were right, but Katherine wanted to see her father pay in a manner that befitted his crimes.

"Fine." Katherine exhaled. "You know where to find me if you need me."

"I do," Jake confirmed.

When Joseph opened the door for them to leave, Katherine moved to the door. However, before she left, she turned back to Rick. "What does this mean for Gabriela Rodriguez?"

"Since she originally discovered the evidence, she's still a material witness. She'll be fine."

Katherine breathed a sigh of relief. She'd known Gabby for most of her life. While living in her parents' house, Gabby had been her only ally. Joseph placed his hand on her lower back and urged her toward the door. "Come on, sweetheart. Let's get out of here."

Katherine nodded. She left the courtroom, relieved she didn't have to testify but upset that her father wasn't truly paying for his sins.

CHAPTER 25

KATHERINE

Joseph pulled into the parking lot and looked over at Katherine with a raised brow. "You ready to knock out this last year?"

Katherine smiled. "So ready."

It was the first day of the fall session and Katherine was looking forward to getting on with her life. Her father's case had been going on for months. So far, there were fifteen plea deals that had culminated from her father's statements. The wheels of justice were turning too slow, but at least the press had eased up. A story about an heiress and her lover, who was also her stepson, killing her husband knocked them right out of the news cycle. Thankfully, they made better news.

Joseph reached over and grabbed her hand. "Sweetheart, how bout we go out to dinner tonight?"

"I would love that." Katherine grinned with mischief on her mind. "And dessert when we get home?"

Joseph reached up and ran his thumb along her jaw. "You read my mind, baby girl."

He hopped out and walked around to open her door. After grabbing their bags from the back seat, he hooked them on his shoulder. Katherine slipped her hand in his and together, they walked hand in hand toward their last year of law school.

JOSEPH

Joseph opened the door and helped Katherine out of the car. For the hundredth time that night, he admired her beauty. Her dark hair flowed over one shoulder and her body was perfection in a fitted black dress. "Have I told you how beautiful you look tonight, Miss Chase?"

She blessed him with a beautiful smile. "Yes, you have, Mr. Storm."

Joseph draped his arm around her. "Let's go in so I can have my dessert."

As they walked arm and arm toward the building, Joseph ran a play-by-play of everything he had planned for his woman. However, when they reached the entrance, they were intercepted by the equivalent of a bucket of cold water.

"Mother, what are you doing here?" Katherine huffed.

Katherine's mother approached with fury and tears in her eyes. "You have destroyed this family!" she spat.

"So, I've heard," Katherine muttered. She moved to walk around her mother, but her mother grabbed her arm and flung her around. She raised her hand to strike Katherine, but Joseph caught her by the wrist. No one, not ever her mother, would ever hurt Katherine again.

"How dare you touch me!" her mother raged. She looked at him like he was beneath her, like his poor hands didn't have the right to touch her rich skin. "Get your hands off me!"

Joseph flung her hand away from Katherine and took a step toward the vile, uppity woman. He made sure to look her directly in the eye. He needed her understand that Katherine was no longer her punching bag.

"Mrs. Chase, please hear me when I tell you that if you ever put your hands on Katherine again, I'm going make you feel pain."

Mrs. Chase's mouth flew open from shock. She looked over at Katherine. "You're going to stand there and let this animal threaten me?"

"Yep. And trust that he means what he says."

Joseph felt Katherine's hand on his back, urging him toward the door. He wrapped his arm around her waist and placed himself between the two women as they walked toward the stairs.

"Your father is dead!" she shouted at their backs.

Katherine froze.

Joseph tried to gauge her reaction, but she had no reaction, not even a hitch in her breathing.

"They're say he hung himself. It's all lies. Your father was only going to serve three years. He would never hang himself."

Katherine took the first step toward their apartment.

"Katherine, they killed him!" her mother cried. "They killed your father!"

Katherine walked up the steps without so much as a glance back at her mother. Joseph unlocked the door and held it open. She stepped into the hall and took the stairs to their apartment.

"They killed your father!" her mother screamed as he closed the door.

Joseph followed Katherine up the stairs and waited for her to unlock the door. After she got it open, they stepped inside. He locked the door, watched her walk over to the sofa, plop down and kick her shoes off.

Joseph took the seat next to her and rubbed her thigh. "Are you okay?"

Katherine sighed. "I am."

She was giving him nothing. He couldn't tell how she was really feeling.

"Are you sure?"

Katherine turned to him and nodded. "I'm sure, honey. I'm absolutely fine. In fact, I feel nothing."

Joseph dropped his head in shame. "You've had to learn to be okay with a lot, sweetheart."

He was partly talking about the fact that he'd killed a man, actually two men.

"Maybe, you're right, honey. But that doesn't change the fact that I am. I'm truly okay."

Joseph pulled Katherine closer and kissed her forehead. "I love you. I hope you know that."

Katherine caressed his jaw and smiled. "I do know that, honey. And I love you too."

KATHERINE

Katherine entered the chapel. She'd arrived two hours early with hopes of not running into anyone. She slowly made her way down the aisle, feeling as if she were walking the plank. When she reached the coffin, she looked down at her father. He was small and gray, not much different than when he was alive.

Katherine didn't know why, but she'd had to see him before they put him in the ground. She'd prayed for his death for years and had waited for the gratification that should have come along with it. Still, she felt nothing but the assurance that he'd never be able to hurt another child.

Proven or not, Katherine believed her mother was right. There's no way her father would've committed suicide. For one, he'd made a sweet deal with the U.S. Attorney.

But ultimately, he'd been too much of a coward to take his own life.

Her father had been preparing to turn on a lot of powerful men. He'd had to die before he reached the top of the food chain.

Katherine gave her father one last glance before walking away, knowing for certain that her father would rot in hell. It was a small consolation, but when she stepped out of that chapel, she knew that she was stepping into a better life. She had a good man who loved her, and he would do anything to keep her safe. For the first time in her life, Katherine was truly happy. The phrase, "Out with the old, in with the new" crossed her mind as she walked down the church steps. That was until she ran right into "the old" on her way down.

"You have some nerve," her mother sneered, walking up the church steps with Maddie in tow.

"Don't have a tizzy, Mother. I just got lost. I'm leaving now."

Since her mother had absolutely no affinity for children, seeing Maddie walking hand in hand with her mother was surprising to say the least. Katherine looked around for her Aunt Evelyn. Surely, she must have been nearby.

"She left," her mother hissed.

Katherine frowned. "What do mean, 'she left'?"

Her mother rolled her eyes. "She said she'd be back in a few weeks."

She moved closer to Maddie and kneeled. "Hey, Maddie."

Maddie looked up with sad eyes. "Hey, Katie."

From such a once vivacious little girl, her timid tone broke Katherine's heart. "Why don't you let her stay with me until Aunt Evelyn comes back?"

Her mother glared at her through hateful, narrowed eyes. "If you think that I would allow you and that brute anywhere near this child, you are insane."

Katherine's eyes flew open. "Oh, wow," she scoffed. She couldn't believe the unmitigated gall of her mother to pretend for one minute that she cared for anyone's well-being besides her own.

"So, she'll be safe with you, huh? You're gonna protect her? That's fucking hilarious! You never protected me. You allowed that man to violate me over and over again!" Katherine ranted. "Thank God he's dead. I hope you follow soon!"

Katherine stormed down the stairs and marched to the car, where her actual protector waited.

NINE MONTHS LATER...
KATHERINE

"I would like to propose a toast," Emily Storm announced.

Katherine stood with the rest of Joseph's family. They'd joined for dinner in celebration of her and Joseph's hooding ceremony. They were finally done with school and soon, they'd be taking the bar exam.

Emily cleared her throat and raised her glass to Joseph. "I just want to say congratulations to my sweet boy. I'm so proud of you. You've always been so focused and determined to reach your goal. For your entire life, if you said it, it was done. You have the biggest heart, and it's filled with love." With tears in her eyes, she turned to Katherine. "That love is for you. I'm so thankful that you entered my son's life. He's the happiest I've ever seen. Congratulations to you. I wish you the best in your career, and I know you're gonna change this world for the better."

Katherine's eyes blurred with tears. "Thank you so much."

"And you," she began, turning to Jonathan. "Good luck on your journey to Italy. Just think... my baby boy will be climbing the ladder in the Lehman Brothers' European division. You've made your mother very proud. I love you, son."

"I love you too, Mom," Jonathon replied.

"Love you, Mom," Joseph concurred.

"I love you too, Emily," Katherine chimed.

"And I love you all," Emily responded with a wide grin. "Cheers!"

"Cheers," Katherine, Jonathan, and Joseph repeated in unison.

They sipped from their glasses and moved to sit.

"Wait!" Joseph blurted, halting their movements. "I also have something to say."

He grabbed Katherine's hand and lifted it to his lips. "I love you," he announced as he dropped to one knee.

Katherine gasped. Her hand flew to her mouth.

"Oh, my God," Emily whispered.

Joseph smiled up at Katherine. In his eyes, she saw a mixture of love and anxiety.

"I need to be with you, in the morning, in the evening. I need to share my life with you because I can't imagine living without you. You give me strength, love, and you soothe the monster in me." Joseph pulled a box from his pocket and flipped it open. Inside was a beautiful, round diamond ring. "Katherine, I need you to be my wife. Will you please do me the honor of being my wife? Sweetheart, will you marry me?"

Katherine swiped tears from her cheeks and nodded. "Yes, Joseph. I'll marry you."

Jonathan clapped and Emily screamed, causing a scene in the dining room of the Cape Cod restaurant.

Joseph slipped the ring onto Katherine's finger and stood. He cupped her face and kissed her tenderly. "Thank you," he whispered.

"I love you," Katherine whispered in return.

Joseph wrapped his arms around her waist and spun her around. "I'm a happy man," he shouted.

The entire restaurant applauded in celebration of their love.

JOSEPH

Joseph poured Katherine a glass of water and grabbed himself a beer out of the refrigerator. When he entered the living room, Katherine was looking down at her ring.

"You've be staring at that ring since I put it on your finger."

"I can't help it, honey. It's so beautiful," she gushed.

"I'm glad you like it."

Joseph sat on the sofa next to her and sip his beer. Katherine looked over at him. Her serious expression was making him nervous.

"Joseph, we need to talk."

Oh shit!

Joseph sat his bottle on the floor and turned to face her. "What's wrong?"

"Well," she sighed. "Even though we're both going to starting new jobs, we'll be starting at the bottom. We really won't have much money. Are you sure you want to get married right now?"

Fear crept into Joseph thoughts. "Have you changed your mind?"

Katherine's eyes grew wide. "God, no, honey." She turned her body and grabbed his hands. "I want to marry you more than anything in the world. I'm just saying, we're kind of broke right now."

Joseph chuckled, feeling a bit of relief. "Katherine, we're not broke. Well... by the standards you were accustomed to, we might be."

"Stop it," Katherine fussed with a laugh.

"Listen, sweetheart. I'm gonna give you the world. I need you to believe that."

Katherine smiled. "I don't need the world. All I need is you."

Joseph cupped the back of her head. "You have me, my love... all of me."

He kissed her lips and turned around to reach for his beer.

"And the baby," she whispered just as he'd taken a sip.

Joseph coughed. Katherine patted his back as he choked on his beer and her news. When he finally recovered, he took a deep breath and turned her way.

"Baby?"

"I'm pregnant, Joseph."

Twice in one day, she'd made him the happiest man in the world. "You're having my baby?"

Katherine nodded and smiled. "Yep."

Joseph's heart swelled. He pulled her into his arms and held on to her for dear life. The thought of starting a family with Katherine filled him with a happiness he wasn't sure he deserved.

He looked at the door. For a brief second, he had a mind to run across the hall to tell Jack his big news. It was what he would have done, had his friend been alive.

"Katherine?"

"Yes?"

"If we have a boy, is it okay if we name him Jackson?"

Katherine pulled out of his arms and caressed his jaw. "Of course. That's a great name for a son."

Joseph sighed with relief. "Thank you."

"I've been thinking about names too."

Joseph raised a brow. "Yeah?"

Katherine nodded. "If we have a girl, I was hoping to name her Emily."

"Really?"

Katherine sighed and rested her head on his chest. "She's the type of woman I'd like my daughter to be like. She's beautiful, smart, hard-working, and she adores her family."

Joseph kissed the top of her head. "I think that's beautiful, sweetheart. I think that's a great idea. But you do realize that you just described yourself as well."

Katherine rubbed his chest. "Aw, honey. Thank you."

Joseph lifted her off his chest and stood. "Come with me," he said, holding out his hand.

She took his hand and stood. "Where are we going?"

Joseph scooped her up into his arms and kissed her lips. "We're going to bed. I need to make love to my fiancée."

Katherine giggled. "The future Mrs. Storm likes the sound of that."

"Mrs. Storm, huh? I really like the sound of *that*."

As Joseph carried his soon-to-be wife down the hall, he couldn't have been more excited about the future.

The End

ABOUT THE AUTHOR

USA TODAY bestselling author, Phoenix Daniels is a novelist who loves creating stories about love, romance, crime, and a ton of sex. She started writing as a tribute to her deceased daughter, Jasmine, whose untimely death interrupted the completion of her first novel. Phoenix wrote her first novel in honor of her fallen angel.

Phoenix Daniels has lived an eventful life and has suffered the greatest of losses. She writes to get through it all. She loves hard and appreciates her "outlets".

As a 22-year veteran of one of the largest police departments in the United States, she has seen and done a great deal in law enforcement, and she often infuses her experiences into her writing. Her men will always be alpha. Her women, strong, kick-ass heroines.

CONNECT WITH PHOENIX DANIELS

Website: mzphoenixdaniels.com

Email: mzphoenixd73@gmail.com

Facebook: https://www.facebook.com/tha.phoenix.1

Facebook page: https://www.facebook.com/AskphoenixD

Facebook group: https://www.facebook.com/groups/291848684331982/

Twitter: https://twitter.com/mzphoenixD

Instagram: https://www.instagram.com/mzphoenixd/

Bookbub: https://www.bookbub.com/authors/phoenix-daniels

Amazon: https://amzn.to/3ooZqRt

Goodreads: https://www.goodreads.com/author/show/6435454.Phoenix_Daniels

PA Name and contact information:

Barbie Pomales

Email Barbiepomales@gmail.com